My tone wasn't e
I could do under the circumstances. "As I said yesterday, I'll call you if I have any questions. But thank you for stopping by in case I needed anything."

I shouldn't really be angry with him. He was a typical prosperous business client who required my services and wanted everything done last week. My frustration came from the pressure he was putting on me along with the backlog of work that had piled up in the two short months since my father died. Fourteen days off to deal with it all was like getting twenty minutes to research an issue for the debate team competition. Insufficient, risky, and courting disaster. Adding to it all my mother's precarious position with regard to finances and a municipal official who held a grudge, I was close to the edge of the cliff.

He studied my face, perhaps searching for some clue as to what I was really thinking, but I hid my exasperation beneath a passive expression.

"Okay, then. Let me know when you hear."

"Of course." I watched him as he strode down the hallway, all long, lean male brimming with the self-assuredness that came from being the heir apparent to a multimillion-dollar redevelopment company. One who could have been on a catwalk in Paris or New York modeling those dark jeans and black pullover that fit him to perfection. An unexpected sigh escaped.

I'd better get my eyes off Mr. Addison's butt and put them on his unsigned contracts.

Praise for Maria Imbalzano

Maria has received many honors for her work including the National Excellence in Story Telling Award, the Heart of Excellence Award and the Write Touch Readers' Award. She was also a finalist for the Readers' Choice Award, the Golden Leaf Award, the RONE Award, and the Book Buyers Best Award.

A SONG FOR ANOTHER DAY
"This book was such a fun, intriguing, captivating, enchanting, romantic, and entertaining read!!! I could not put this book down—nor did I want to."

~Fabulous and Brunette Blog
~*~

THE BLUEBERRY SWIRL WALTZ
"This fast paced and easily readable story is a delight… By her talent in creating dialogue and voice, author Imbalzano's talents clearly extend to creating a setting which takes one back to a small riverside town… Ahh, the memories."

~Kat Henry Doran, Wild Women Reviews
~*~

SWORN TO FORGET
"Nicki and Dex have amazing chemistry and their heat is scorching, both in and out of the bedroom."

~LJT, NetGalley reviewer
~*~

RED VELVET CRINKLES AND CHRISTMAS SPRINKLES
"A delight to read…this book is a star above the rest…a must read."

~Still Moments Magazine

Return to Wylder

by

Maria Imbalzano

The Wylder West

Return to Wylder

Cover Art by *Diana Carlile*

The Wild Rose Press, Inc.
PO Box 708
Adams Basin, NY 14410-0708
Visit us at www.thewildrosepress.com

Publishing History
First Edition, 2022
Trade Paperback ISBN 978-1-5092-4313-6
Digital ISBN 978-1-5092-4314-3

The Wylder West
Published in the United States of America

Dedication

To my beautiful mom,
who is one of the strongest women I know.
Thank you for your love and support
throughout the years.

Chapter One
Emma Jane

"That's impossible. You can't take two weeks off."
Lynne Carrington, the head of our law firm's
commercial real estate department, didn't look up at me
from the contract she studied, her red marker
underlining, slashing, and commenting all over the
page. "The Briar closing is in a month, and I need your
help." She looked up. "You know how important you
are to me and to the firm. Besides, you just had a
vacation."

I had requested three weeks, not two, and the
vacation I'd just had was eight weeks ago in early
March when I attended my father's funeral in my
hometown of Wylder, Wyoming. It had been one of the
saddest and most emotional times of my life—not
exactly a frivolous getaway.

I couldn't back down. "I'm sorry, Lynne, but I
have to go home. My father's law firm requires
attention. I either have to hire another lawyer to help
the associate there or find a buyer. My mom needs me.
I can't help from here."

"Why can't the associate do it?" Her impatience
came through in a glare.

"He's only been there a year, and he doesn't have
the experience or the time to deal with it. From what
my mother tells me, he's putting out fires left and right,

but many of their cases are falling between the cracks."

My chest tightened, and my heart ached over my dogged resistance to Dad's request that I return home to practice law with him. I'd always told myself I would in the future, after enough time had gone by to dull the pain keeping me away. But as each year passed, another excuse arose. *I'm learning so much here in San Francisco, and it will help in the long run. I'm in the middle of a huge real estate deal which will take at least six to nine more months. I'm committed to coaching the moot court team at Berkeley Law.* The real reason never crossed my lips.

Lynne still hadn't put down her pen or acknowledged the seriousness of my problem. But my boss had major multitasking skills and could listen and work at the same time, so I continued. "It may not be the ideal time, but there's never a good time." I exhaled loudly, trying to lasso her waning focus. "I have to go. There's no other option. Some major client, Dylan Addison, is apparently demanding more attention than he's getting. I have to make sure he doesn't jump ship and retain other counsel. His business is important to the firm."

Finally, Lynne looked up, her eyebrow practically touching her hairline. "Dylan Addison of Addison Redevelopment Corp.?"

"Yes. Why? Do you know him?"

"I know of the company. His father, Deacon Addison, started the business thirty years ago, and now it's huge. Mostly taking on projects in Chicago, but I wouldn't be surprised if they expanded into other big cities. How did your father land such a prominent client?"

"I have no idea, but I guess I'll find out when I get there." I made this last statement with confidence, as if Lynne had already given me the go-ahead to leave.

Silence descended upon us. I could wait her out. I'd worked with the woman for six years. Intimidation was her trademark, but I was immune to her ploys. I'd even channeled her unsettling stare at negotiations.

"Two weeks. And you'll work from there. This Briar closing is a bear, and the work can't stop just because you're traipsing off to some tiny hamlet in Wyoming."

I ignored her flawed depiction of my trip since I was winning this battle of wills. "Of course I'll work from Wylder. Ron Briar knows how to reach me, and I have all his contact information."

He called at least five times a day with questions and demands, disregarding the hour as if nine p.m. were as acceptable as nine a.m. His feeling of entitlement aggravated me on several levels. A vice president at his father's commercial real estate company, he lorded over all his associates and colleagues as if they were his slaves. And rules of civility didn't seem to apply to him. The words *please, thank you, I'm sorry to bother you,* or *is it too late to call* were missing from his vocabulary. But he was an important client who spent a fortune in legal fees, so I had to bite my tongue and yes him to death.

Although I'd agreed to Lynne's terms, I honestly didn't know how I could possibly work from Wylder when I'd be reviewing every one of my father's files and determining the next step for his law firm. It was a daunting job if given a month, yet I'd barely managed to eke out two weeks. While still working on the Briar case.

As if she could read my mind, she gave me an assessing look before changing the subject. "Pick up or download a copy of the latest issue of *Business USA* and read it on the plane."

Was that a smirk on her mouth? I was a second away from asking her why but didn't want to give her more time to back down on her stingy and lukewarm deal granting me time away. The magazine had probably run a story about one of our major clients.

Carter, Masters, and Smith was a prestigious mid-size law firm in San Francisco, and I was lucky to have such a great job working with huge developers. Commercial real estate in the city was ripe with legal issues, and my plate was full at all times—a good thing in my quest to learn as much as possible about every aspect of real estate law. This career choice had bolstered my confidence with the added benefit that if or when I decided to join my father, I'd be an expert in my field. Except that now my move would never happen.

"Thanks, Lynne. I'm leaving first thing tomorrow morning."

She grunted, already disconnected from our conversation and back working on the contract she'd been reviewing. I turned on my heel and left without waiting for another possible contingency to interfere with my plan.

****

On Tuesday morning, as I drove my rental car from the Cheyenne airport toward Wylder, conflicting emotions bombarded my brain. I was returning for more than my usual long weekend or holiday visit. This place had been my home, a small town where its innate comradery was fostered by monthly community gatherings big and small: the Spring Festival, the Fourth of July celebration, the Harvest Ball, seasonal dances, and various potluck dinners and picnics. I'd known every business owner and their families, from the shops in town to the ranches and farms just outside its borders. I'd also known the teachers, coaches, ranch hands, and sales people.

And they all knew me as one of Hank Hampton's daughters.

The one who was still alive.

Despite all the happy memories of my twin sister and me growing up, I'd unraveled when Ashley died at age eighteen. I was her best friend, and she was mine. We had planned our future careers together while huddling under the sheets when we were supposed to be sleeping. Ashley and EJ, future attorneys-at-law, who would join our father and make it a formidable family firm.

Even now, after thirteen years had passed since she left me, I still had a huge hole in my heart. Sure, the acute pain had dissipated, with time being the age-old healer. And living and working in San Francisco kept the tangible memories at bay. But every time I returned home, my heart twisted, and it didn't uncoil until I escaped the town limits.

I opened the window and inhaled the fresh, clean air of this early May day. The terrain opened up outside Cheyenne, and the rolling, grassy plains were painted with every color green imaginable—emerald, kelly, chartreuse, sage, turquoise, and forest. Dry prairies of dusty sand and red earth competed with the greenery, decorated with shrub-steppe and sagebrush. Rocky, jagged mountains rose in the distance with snow still evident on the higher peaks as they reached for the clear blue sky. The beauty of Wyoming would never get old, and I appreciated it even more now that I was no longer a resident.

I drove into Wylder along the railroad tracks and passed the train station, which still had hitching posts for the horses—an attraction loved by tourists. The Five Star Saloon sat across the street, weathered with stories of brawls and gun battles back in the day. Now it was a respectable establishment with karaoke on some nights and line dancing on others. In the next block stood Joe's Barber Shop, a meeting place for many of the local men who gossiped just as fiercely as the women at Artistic Hair Salon. I passed the Chamber of Commerce building where Mom worked—or more candidly volunteered—as the director of events.

Reaching the corner of Buckboard Alley and Wylder Street, I came to the familiar site of Dad's law office—a two-story, red-brick and cement structure, looking solid and sturdy. A mahogany sign with gold lettering hung above the first story—*The Law Office of Hank Hampton*. Without warning, tears flooded my eyes. I now had another trauma to suffer.

I parked behind the building, then took a few tentative steps toward the office I knew so well, attempting to remove all evidence of my waterworks, but a new torrent threatened to spill down my face. I inhaled deeply, blinked several times, and threw my shoulders back. Then I entered the building. I could do this.

"Hi, Carol." I stood before my father's long-time

secretary and receptionist, the woman who was the glue, backbone, and face of the practice.

"EJ!" She jumped up from her desk, her perfect blonde pageboy not moving an inch as she gave me a huge hug. "I'm so glad you're here."

"That's quite a reception. Thank you." I paused and studied her face. More lines than I'd remembered creased her forehead. "Are you okay?"

Her lips turned down. "I miss your dad. He was such an amazing man to work for." Tears shone in her kind, brown eyes. "But it was his time to leave us." She glanced around, presumably to assure that no one else could hear our conversation, but no clients occupied the reception area. She whispered anyway. "Bryce is in over his head. He only worked for your dad for a year, and now he's in charge." A grimace furrowed her brow. "He can't keep up. Your dad had some big cases, some important clients."

"I read about Dylan Addison in *Business USA*." Dylan, the heir apparent to Addison Redevelopment, ran among the elite circles in Chicago society. Several photos had shown him to be quite the celebrity magnet, with a well-known lingerie model on his arm at a Red Cross gala, an ingénue linking arms with him as they strolled through the Magnificent Mile section of the city, and a bikini-clad beauty sailing beside him on Lake Michigan. What in the world was he doing in Wylder? "My mother told me he's a client. What is the firm doing for him?"

"He recently bought the Wylder Hotel. Although he's tried to be patient after your father died, his tolerance is fading. If he doesn't get the representation he needs, he's going to leave. I'm afraid other clients are in the same situation. If this keeps up, the business will be worth nothing, and I know your mom is counting on her share of the income to get by."

"She did say she was a little worried, which is why I'm here." While I'd had a brief talk with Mom about the issues cropping up, I hadn't gotten the impression it was quite as dire as Carol was now portraying.

"I'm sorry to burden you with all this the second you get here, but Mr. Addison has an appointment with Bryce at ten thirty this morning, and Bryce is still in court."

I glanced at my watch. Ten twenty. "Well, I guess I'll meet with him, but you better give me some details before I jump into the fire."

The creases in Carol's forehead disappeared, and the beginning of a smile emerged. "I can't tell you how relieved I am that you're here—for whatever time you can give us. Your office is all set up down the hall across from your father's."

"My office?"

"Yes. Your dad furnished it a few years ago so it would be ready when you joined him."

A ball of pain stuck in my throat. He'd been waiting so patiently, never pushing, only asking when I might make the move. He'd clearly thought it would have happened sooner.

Just then the door opened, and a tall, broad-shouldered, extremely handsome man—definitely the icon from the magazine—walked in. He wore designer jeans, a pale-blue cashmere sweater, black sports coat, and a gold Rolex heavy enough to weigh his arm down.

A small sigh came from Carol before she whispered, "That's him."

Mr. Dylan Addison in the flesh, minus the woman of the day. Looking every bit as gorgeous and wealthy as he had in print. "I'm Emma Jane Hampton." I stuck out my hand to shake his. "Hank Hampton's daughter."

"Great." A dazzling smile accompanied his words. "I'm glad I'll finally have the representation I need. Your father spoke very highly of you. I'm sure you'll be able to get the necessary permits immediately now that you're taking over."

My breath caught for the few seconds it took to come up with a response that would keep him as a client but disavow him of his mistaken belief that I was taking over. "I'm here for a few weeks to help out." No use stating that it was only two, and my main goal was to review the caseload and determine the next phase, not step into my father's shoes and represent clients. Best to find out exactly what Mr. Addison needed before bursting his balloon or sending him scurrying to another law firm. Plus, curiosity had me in its grip.

"Let's go into my office and talk." I headed toward the back of the building where my father's office occupied one corner and a fully furnished unoccupied office sat across the hall. Floor-to-ceiling windows overlooked a small park-like area with lush green grass, two maple trees for shade, and colorful flowers just blooming for spring.

I switched on the light and glanced around, explaining the office's lack of files and other missing evidence of being a work space. "I only arrived a few minutes ago. I flew in from San Francisco this morning, so I'm not familiar with your case."

"It's good to know you have your father's work ethic."

Before I faced him from behind my desk, I inhaled for the tact I'd require to delicately balance his needs against mine. "Have a seat, Mr. Addison."

"Please call me Dylan." He sat, crossing an ankle over his knee. "Emma Jane or EJ?" he asked.

"Ms. Hampton is good."

His Adam's apple rose and fell in his throat as crystal-blue eyes studied me.

I laughed, coyly acknowledging that I'd knocked the playboy a little off-balance. "Kidding. EJ is fine."

His slow-forming grin told me he wasn't quite sure how to take me. No need to explain. I wouldn't be here long enough for him to get to know me anyway.

"So how can I help you?"

Normally, I would have pulled a legal pad and pen in front of me to take notes, but since I wouldn't be doing whatever it was he needed, I'd simply get the gist and pass it on to Bryce who probably already knew what wasn't getting done.

"Your father represented me in purchasing the Wylder Hotel at the end of February. Since he knew all the players in town, he told me it would be easy to get the approvals I need to renovate the place. The general contractor filed the paperwork for the permits, but we just received this letter that there are problems. It says I'm required to get a variance." He removed a folded letter from inside his jacket pocket and handed it to me. "Construction has to start now. I don't have time to apply for a variance. Hank led me to believe that if an issue arose, he would take care of it." He paused, shifting in his chair. "I'm very sorry about your father's passing, EJ. I'm guessing it was quite a shock."

"Thank you." The muscles in my throat tightened,

and I didn't want to encourage a flood of tears, so staying away from the subject worked best. "I'll speak to Bryce and see if he could talk to the person in charge to push this through." Hopefully, that would keep Dylan at the firm for any further legal work he would need to get the hotel up and running. "If we have any problem, we'll give you a call." I studied his demeanor. Calm but no-nonsense, civil but straight to the point. "I'm curious. Why did you buy the Wylder Hotel? You're headquartered in Chicago, and from what I've read, your company takes on much larger projects in big cities."

"Reading up on me, huh?" His brow arched, and cool blue eyes flashed.

"I just happened to scan the latest issue of *Business USA* on the plane. Coincidently, you were featured." I didn't tell him that my boss had suggested it as required reading after I mentioned his name.

His smile seemed to ooze satisfaction. I had no tolerance for arrogance and didn't have time to feed his ego. He had better not be another Ron Briar—entitled, rude, and demanding. Two at the same time might just push me over the edge. I stood, indicating our meeting was over despite not receiving an answer to my question about his motives in purchasing the Wylder Hotel.

But he continued to sit, his eyes locking on mine. "I want you to work on this project, not Bryce. He's a good guy, but he doesn't have the experience needed to represent me or my business interests. There are several contracts I sent over here for review, and I haven't heard a word."

Appeasing him was going to be harder than I'd

imagined. "I'll be here to help him with any questions he has." I'd also find out from Bryce why he wasn't getting the work done for a major client.

"I've been very patient, knowing how difficult it's been with your father's passing. But Bryce is more of a litigator, and that's not what I need. I know you work on huge real estate deals in San Francisco. I'm sure my needs will be easy for you to handle. If you tell me you don't have time, then I'll look for new representation." Gone was the half-hearted smile and in its place a hard jaw tensing with displeasure.

I could not let him leave the firm. Keeping clients, especially key ones, would increase the value of the firm in case a sale was necessary. I needed to figure out what Dylan required in terms of legal work and have a sit down with Bryce to determine if he could in fact handle it. If not, I'd cover it while here and possibly even from San Francisco. "I'll review your file and see what I could do."

"Great." Dylan finally stood. "I'd appreciate knowing if we have to apply for a variance by tomorrow. Of course, I'm counting on you to convince the powers that be that it's not necessary."

Not too much pressure. But making it happen would be in my best interests as well. If I had to apply for a variance, I'd have to then attend the next planning board meeting, and who knew how often those happened in Wylder.

I walked him to the front of the office, and he shook my hand, the warmth of his clasped fingers around mine sending heat and sparks up my arm. He held it a little too long, a little too intimately. I connected with his eyes, expecting to see a teasing flicker—one that he no doubt used on his adoring models to show his playful side. Instead I saw an intensity that arrowed strait to my core.

Backing away, I severed our bond and glanced around the reception area where five people were waiting. Dylan gave me a look that I interpreted as *good luck.* Ignoring him and finding my smile, I introduced myself to the waiting clients before stating I'd be right back. I nodded for Carol to follow me and pulled her into the empty conference room.

"Why didn't you warn me that Dylan Addison is a difficult client?" Was that the correct label for him, or was it more like disturbing—as in unsettling all my cells?

"He only became difficult when his needs stopped being met. I didn't get a chance to tell you much about him before he showed up. Bad timing."

I shook my head. "I'm sorry. But I've only been here for a half hour, and he's managed to dump his entire case on me." As well as his aura invading my personal space. "He doesn't want Bryce to work on it. And what's going on out there?" I jabbed my finger toward the reception area.

"It's like this every day. Clients have appointments, but Bryce can't always make them. Today he's caught up in court on a DUI."

Those three little letters—driving under the influence—froze my limbs. I could feel the blood drain from my head, and I grasped for a nearby chair for support.

"Are you okay?" Carol took hold of my arm and directed me to sit.

"I'm...I'm fine. I just got a little dizzy. I didn't eat

anything for breakfast." That sounded rational.

Because it certainly wasn't rational that I could still become completely overwhelmed thirteen years later when the letters DUI were mentioned. Had all that therapy done nothing?

"Sit for a few minutes. I'll get you some orange juice and see if we have any protein bars in the kitchen."

As soon as she left, I inhaled a huge breath and let it out slowly. My sister's face floated before me, compassionate and understanding. I reached out to touch her, but she faded away. Beautiful, ethereal Ashley. Her life cut short by a drunk driver.

Carol handed me a glass of juice. "I'll run to the diner and get you a muffin." She studied me. "Bryce just called. He said he should be back in forty-five minutes, but he has two more matters in court this afternoon. Do you think you could handle the clients out there?" Her eyes begged me to take care of my father's business.

I bowed my head and sighed. I hadn't counted on meeting with clients and actually doing legal work while I was here. I'd intended to get the files in order so Mom could make an informed decision about hiring another lawyer or selling the business. Yet I couldn't let all those people sit there without at least finding out what they wanted.

I inhaled a breath, straightened my shoulders, and headed into the reception area.

"Okay. Who's first?"

Chapter Two
Dylan

An unnamed energy buzzed through me as I opened and closed my fist, still feeling the remnants of EJ's heat coursing through my veins. A slow smile tugged at my lips. A surprising turn of events. Not only did I luck out that a competent real estate attorney had finally arrived to help at Hank's firm, but it happened to be EJ Hampton, an expert in the field and a force to be reckoned with.

Hank had often talked about his daughter, who had a great job at a San Francisco firm, gaining invaluable experience for when she'd come home and work with him. It was tragic that her father had died so suddenly—before the move happened—but maybe now that she was here, she'd reevaluate and return to Wylder. This town could certainly use someone with her expertise. And Hank had a great practice that she could step into. A win for her. And definitely a win for me and my legal needs.

Although I'd seen her photo in Hank's office, she was more striking in person. Long, golden-brown hair cascaded around her shoulders, and those stunning sapphire eyes almost looked navy. Their uniqueness had stolen my focus until I realized it and tore my gaze away so as not to appear rude. The serious set of her jaw while listening to my demands had softened when I gave her my condolences over losing her father, drawing attention to her vulnerability. Yet she'd cloaked herself in armor to keep her sadness at bay—the consummate professional.

Just what I needed to get those permits, which would allow me to start renovations on the hotel.

My cell phone buzzed, and I checked the screen to identify the caller. My father. I blew out a breath and answered. "Hi, Dad. What's up?"

"I've called you three times over the past two days, and you haven't responded to any of my messages." The scolding in his voice couldn't be missed. Did he chastise other vice presidents at the company with the same disparaging tone, or was that reserved for me?

"Sorry. I've been busy."

"When you convinced me to take on this project because you thought it would be good to diversify our portfolio, I reluctantly agreed. You promised me this renovation would only take a few months and we'd be seeing profits before the end of the year. Since March, there's been no movement. What the hell is going on?" His anger built with each sentence.

"I already told you my lawyer died unexpectedly, and we recently ran into a snag in getting the permits."

"Then get another lawyer. Preferably from Cheyenne where the firms are bigger and can handle our needs. Pronto."

I shouldn't have answered his call. He continually interfered, questioning my judgment, demanding that issues be handled his way. And of course, I bristled. "Hank's daughter just came back to town from San Francisco. She's a big-time real estate attorney there with the experience we need. She'll be able to put this project back on track." At least I hoped so.

When I arrived in Wylder in January, I hadn't been sure this was the place to buy. It was a sleepy town of roughly four thousand residents, and by the looks of its buildings and environs, change wasn't in their vocabulary. But once I'd met Hank Hampton, the decision was easy. Hank took me around town and showed me the lay of the land, the entire time listing the pros—and to be fair, the cons—of purchasing the Wylder Hotel. It had been empty for the past two years, and the price was right. The perfect project to prove to Dad that small-town renovations would enhance our business and add a layer of depth.

Hank was the consummate professional in dealing with the negotiations leading up to the closing on the hotel, and he promised to work with me on all my legal needs involving the property. He was not only my lawyer, but had become my friend.

And then he'd died while sitting at his desk working—a massive heart attack the culprit.

If that didn't caution people, myself included, to enjoy life to its fullest every day, then nothing would.

Which pushed me even harder to make this small-town venture work. I wasn't cut out to take charge of any of the huge development deals my father favored in Chicago. My heart wasn't in those projects. Redesigning or redeveloping huge multistory buildings to add more office space or more hotel rooms to already burgeoning cities held no satisfaction. Fulfillment came from making a difference. At least in my book.

My father continued. "If things don't start moving by the end of the month, I'm pulling you off this project. We'll sell the building as is and get out of town. Do you understand?"

"Perfectly." Bile rose in my throat, and my jaw ached as my teeth clenched. "I'll send you an email with our progress." Talking to him by phone just sent my stress level to the moon.

I disconnected and walked down the street with no destination in mind—just a leisurely stroll to clear my head of Dad's demands before moving on to my next meeting. I knew I could win him over. If I was successful in this venture.

Regrettably, my legal and personal counselor was gone, and problem after problem arose. I didn't want to leave the firm, knowing that Hank's wife depended on part of the income from the business to sustain her. Yet Bryce Seward was not the attorney for me. He knew nothing about real estate law and had his hands full trying to keep the firm afloat.

Although my father's directive was clear, I didn't want to hire a firm from Cheyenne. If my goal was to renovate the Wylder Hotel, which in turn would invigorate the town and help its businesses, I had to hire local architects, plumbers, electricians. And lawyers. I'd researched the lawyers in town before I chose to invest here, but only Hank could have met my needs.

And now, it was only EJ.

Chapter Three
Emma Jane

I handed Carol the redwell filled with paper documents from my last appointment. No computer files here.

Carol exhaled. "You're a lifesaver."

I smiled at the woman who had been my dad's right hand—at least in the office. "Thanks for smoothing the way today."

I'd met with everyone who showed up, giving them only a half hours' time before shooing them out the door with a promise to do what needed to be done. It wasn't a bad way to learn about my father's open cases. He'd done wills, trusts, real estate closings, incorporations of small businesses, and whatever else those areas touched upon. He'd been a transactional lawyer and had only gone to court if an already existing client got a traffic ticket. Not until Bryce came had the office begun representing clients for all matters involving litigation.

Dad's practice thrived despite his antiquated systems. Sure, he and his secretary had computers, but he had none of the case management or billing systems that most law firms relied upon. He'd resisted those programs when I suggested them, telling me *it was all up here* as he pointed to his head.

For most of his legal career, he'd been a solo

practitioner in Wylder, representing his clients the old-fashioned way—usually talking to them in person but on the phone in a pinch. Everything he discussed with them was followed up by a memo to the file, dictated to his secretary, and sometimes a letter memorializing the terms agreed upon. Communicating by email was a sacrilege—a sin he would never commit.

A true gentleman and advocate for his clients, my father had an exceptional reputation. He worked five days a week, eleven hours a day—from seven to six—golfed on Saturday mornings, weather permitting, and spent the rest of the weekend with my mom. No matter how busy he got, he refused to hire a lawyer to lessen his burden—until last year.

He must have realized that my rationalizations for staying in San Francisco could go on for years, so he'd finally caved due to the mounting pressure of his caseload.

My chest ached, and my throat constricted over my excuse-laden refusal to come back home to practice law. I could have been here for him the last few years of his life, making him happy, his dream fulfilled. Mine too, if I'd allowed it.

How could I have let Ashley's death destroy my lifelong goal to work side by side with Dad? The short answer—I'd done it because it was as much Ashley's ambition as it was mine and our father's. I had permitted my loyalty to her to eclipse my loyalty to him.

A heavy sigh escaped.

I glanced at my watch. Three thirty. I pulled Dylan's file, which had a copy of the permit applications, and breezed through them. After grabbing that folder as well as the letter setting forth the problem, I headed toward the front door.

"Carol, I'm going to the municipal building. I hope to be back soon."

I walked the three blocks to the town's offices and found the permit office with no trouble. Thankfully, no one else was waiting for help—not a surprise—and I strode up to the counter.

A man about my age approached, his shirt sleeves rolled up and his tie askew. "How can I help you?" he asked, although his tone did not connote a warm welcome.

"I'm Emma Jane Hampton, Hank Hampton's daughter." I hoped that would pave the way and be all I needed to get past any problem. "We represent Dylan Addison, who received this letter." I pulled it out and handed it to him.

"Well, well. If it isn't EJ Hampton coming into my domain to discuss a problem."

I scanned his face for recollection since he obviously knew who I was. Then it hit me. "Adam Colton? I haven't seen you since high school. How are you?"

This couldn't be happening. We hadn't exactly been friends even though we were on the debate team together. He'd blamed me for losing the state championship senior year. I'd been a mess since Ashley died and shouldn't have even been on the team, but Mr. Hermann probably didn't want to mess me up even more than I already was by making me sit out.

Adam's tone held something close to hostility. "Your client needs a variance to increase the size of the kitchen at the hotel."

I tacked on a smile, hoping it looked genuine. "He's not really increasing the size of the kitchen. He simply needs to add more storage space for a pantry and a second industrial refrigerator. It's hardly worth going through the variance process." I laughed, hoping to show how frivolous that would be. "The legal work involved, the meeting of the planning board, the time wasted... I was hoping you could waive this trivial objection to the permits, given this very minor addition to a huge hotel."

He wasn't smiling back.

"Rules are rules." He shook his head as if there were nothing he could do, but I knew better.

"Yes, but I'm guessing this town could use more tourism, and in order to get it, those tourists need a nice place to stay. Mr. Addison has plans to market the hotel and the town once the renovations are complete." At least I hoped he would. "You don't want to hold up something that will benefit the town, do you? For a storage room?"

"You may recall, Emma Jane, that we were on the debate team together senior year, and we lost a major debate because you didn't follow the rules."

Of course he would remember. I'd misjudged the time allotted for research, and we'd been disqualified from the final round of competition. Ignoring the haze of embarrassment over that little debacle, I spoke with my silkiest voice as if it were a trivial matter.

"Adam, that was a long time ago. And it was just a high school debate. This is much more serious. Obtaining a variance will cost my client money and time he doesn't have. The permits have already been held up for two months pending review. It doesn't make sense to hold them up another two months because of this tiny addition. Will you please consider waiving this requirement?"

Seconds went by in silence as he studied the rejection letter. Was he wavering? "I'll think about it."

Exasperation filled every pore. "For how long?" If it took too long, I'd be wasting precious days in not filing for the variance when in the end, I might have to file for it anyway. "I don't have time to play this game."

As soon as the words spilled from my mouth, I knew I'd made an error.

"It's not a game. You need to learn how things work around here. Stop by on Friday afternoon, and I'll give you my final answer."

I felt like I was on a game show. "That's two days from now!" The volume of my voice rose with my frustration, and I feared it came out too chastising. I grasped for some honey to pour over my words. "What about tomorrow?"

"You're pushing it, EJ. If you want me to look at this favorably, you should be nicer. Like your father was."

That stung. "Would you have waived the requirement for him?"

"He was a great guy. We worked together to get things done in this town."

Not exactly an answer, but I took it to mean he would have. I bit my tongue and tried to come at the problem from a different angle. "Dylan Addison was my father's client. I'm just here to give my father's clients the representation they would have gotten from him. So if you would have allowed the permits to go through for my dad, why can't you let them go through for his client?"

Would he bend if I took myself out of the mix?

His brow furrowed. "I didn't say I would have issued the permits for your dad. I said we worked together to get things done. You and I have no working relationship. You're an out-of-towner."

These last words smacked me in the face. Was I really an out-of-towner just because I'd worked in San Francisco for the last six years? My college and law school years away shouldn't count. And I had intended to come back…someday.

Adam broke into my thoughts. "As I said, I'll let you know on Friday. Be here at two." With that he turned and disappeared down the hall.

Great. I'd been in Wylder for less than a day and already been labeled a rule breaker, an outsider, and lacking the nice gene by someone who could be instrumental in burying me and Dylan in paperwork and process while construction lay dormant.

Adam was right about one thing. I'd better learn how to curry favor with the locals by immersing myself back into the community if I intended to help my mother's situation instead of hurt it.

Even if I had no intention of returning permanently.

****

"Hi, Mom. I'm home." I slipped through the front door, pulling my luggage and computer case in my wake.

"Hi, Emma Jane. I'm in the kitchen."

My mom always called me by my full name upon first arriving. After that I was simply EJ.

"It smells good in here. What are you making?" I went over and gave her a kiss and a hug.

"Pot roast and potatoes. I figured you could use a good home-cooked meal tonight after the full day you've had. I wish you would have stopped by here this morning after your flight instead of going straight to the office."

Old habits died hard, and I went directly to the refrigerator to see if there was anything interesting to nibble on or to drink. I found an unopened bottle of wine, and my mood rose with the discovery. "Sorry. I wanted to get started right away. I could only take two weeks off." Holding the bottle of Chardonnay aloft, I asked, "Shall we splurge tonight since you went to all this trouble to make dinner? I have to work on one of my cases later, but a glass can't hurt."

"Sure. You know where the corkscrew is."

I located two stemmed glasses in the cupboard, removed the cork, and poured some wine before sitting at the counter. "Do you need any help?"

"It's all under control. The guest house is made up for you. Or you could sleep in your old bedroom."

"The guest house would be great. That way I can work well into the night without disturbing your routine." And I wouldn't have to worry about falling out of the single bed that still lived in my old room.

"How was it at the office today?" My mother's brow creased, and the heartache from losing the love of her life so suddenly was etched on her face. It had only been two months, but I prayed my mom would find joy again.

"I'm afraid I have a daunting task in front of me. I didn't get a chance to start analyzing the files yet since

I met with clients all day. That place is a revolving door."

"Your father had an excellent reputation around town. His clients loved him."

"Yes. Everyone I met with had nothing but nice things to say about him. And they all felt like they knew me. Whether from my younger days or Dad talking their ears off about me, I don't know." They'd been so trusting, content to transfer their faith and loyalty in my dad to me. For however short a time I'd be here.

I should have come clean to Dad. Told him the real reason I couldn't return. Ashley had been such a big part of my hopes and dreams to practice law in Wylder. When we were young and our dad would take us to the office on Saturdays so Mom could have some time to herself, we'd sit in the conference room with one of us pretending to be the client and the other the lawyer. The lawyer would take notes on yellow legal pads with red and blue markers, then hole-punch them and insert them into a file folder. Eventually, we'd migrate to the reception area and write up fake messages about would-be callers. Ashley had even designed a logo for when the firm would be changed to Hampton, Hampton, and Hampton.

If Dad had known about my mental block, perhaps he would have been able to talk me through it—convince me that I wouldn't be betraying her by joining him. Then we could have practiced law together, as we'd always discussed.

But fate jumped in, and the burden I carried around, the burden that had kept me from buying into his dream, now seemed senseless.

Mom's smile appeared. "He was so proud of you.

And he let everyone in town know it. I am too, honey."

The ball in my throat rebounded, this time a little more painful because I was sharing a moment with my mom and not a stranger. I nodded, fighting to keep the tears at bay.

The time had come to talk about the present. "We spoke a little on the phone about Dad's will and what your options are with regard to the firm. You can either take twenty-five percent of the net monthly proceeds or sell it."

Mom nodded. "I've been so conflicted. I hate the thought of ending your father's legacy. He put so much of himself into the business. But I don't see how the firm can continue to run without selling it. I'm sure you saw that Bryce can't handle it all."

I was grateful my mother didn't verbalize her belief that I was her only hope of keeping the business afloat and continuing my father's legacy. But even though she didn't lend voice to that opinion, it circled around me like a rope, threatening to tether me.

Famous for ignoring anything I didn't want to acknowledge, I stuck to my script. "I did notice that Bryce is overwhelmed. I wanted to talk to him, but he was in court most of the day and then left by the time I got back from…a meeting." Not wanting to add more angst to my mom's plate, I omitted discussing specific legal problems and focused on the practice in general. "Have you spoken to Bryce about hiring another lawyer, or does he want to leave?" It dawned on me that he might not want to stay since his practice was totally different from my dad's.

"I talked to him, suggesting he hire someone else with more experience to help out. But he said it would be next to impossible to find someone to take your father's place. It would have to be an attorney from out of town since all the lawyers in Wylder already have their own practices. And he'd have to find someone with years of experience in the same areas as your father. I agree such a person would not be easy to find."

"Then your only other option is to sell." If I looked at this pragmatically through my attorney eyes and not through an emotional prism, I could set the wheels in motion. "In order to sell, we'll need Bryce to stay on to work on the current cases so the business retains its value. If Dad's clients don't get the service they require, they'll leave and go elsewhere. Then the business won't be worth anything."

The lines bracketing Mom's mouth deepened. "I need the money from the law firm to survive. You know how little I make at the Chamber of Commerce."

"Don't you and Dad have other assets, life insurance?" Surely, my mom couldn't be relying solely on money from the law practice.

"Some. We own the building that the law office is in, and your father invested in a few other businesses around town."

My stomach sank. The businesses in Wylder were not much to speak of. "What businesses?" I held my breath.

"He has an interest in the Vincent House Hotel & Restaurant, as well as the movie theater and Jake's Place. I believe there are three other partners involved."

At least they were all thriving businesses after going through some hard times. I remembered my dad mentioning that some of the main businesses in town needed a cash infusion if they were going to survive.

He must have put a partnership together to assure those mainstays continued. But those interests were not going to turn into cash anytime soon. All of my father's partners would have to agree to sell or buy his interest out. I'd need to focus on the law practice.

"I can research business evaluators from the area when I get to the office tomorrow and speak to Dad's accountant and some realtors about the potential sale of the practice and building." I'd start with the local professionals since they'd know who the likely players would be in or near Wylder.

"Do you think the practice could be sold for a fair price? Your father always had a lot of clients, but he didn't always press them for payment. Especially during some of the bad financial times we've had here. There's probably a lot of accounts receivable on the books. Legal bills that will never get paid."

Dad had been a benevolent advocate, sympathetic to those who were having trouble making ends meet. He wouldn't turn them away if they needed legal help, even if they couldn't pay. Running a small-town firm was part legal work and part social work, a service my firm in San Francisco would never provide.

I hoped the law firm was healthy enough to garner a good price. "I guess we'll find out. In the meantime, I'll talk to Bryce to see what he needs in the short run to keep the business running smoothly and successfully." I gulped the rest of my wine, hoping the alcohol would dull the headache creeping into my temples. "Let's eat. I have work to do, or I won't have a job to go back to."

The daunting tasks before me seemed overwhelming. I'd just have to take one step at a time without looking at the avalanche rushing toward me. I

could do this.
    I had to.
    My mother needed the money.

Chapter Four
Emma Jane

"What do you know about Dylan Addison's case?" I was meeting with Bryce first thing Wednesday morning, with the goal of reviewing every case in the office to see which ones needed immediate attention. My secondary reason was to start evaluating the worth of those cases for a potential sale.

Bryce groaned. "He needs the construction permits. He paid your father a huge retainer to do all the legal work necessary to get the Wylder Hotel up and running again."

"We hit a bump. Dylan received a letter from the permit department that the permits are being held up until he applies for a variance for the storage area he's adding on."

"That's not good. Your father told him his application would go through without a variance."

Of course he did. "My father knew all the players at the municipal building, and apparently, he was able to deal with them because of his personal relationships. I went down there yesterday to try to push it through, and Adam Colton, the permit officer, initially said the rules are the rules and we need a variance. When I pressed him, he said he'd think about it and let me know on Friday. Do you know Adam?"

"A little. From around town. Seems like a nice guy.

Real estate is not my area of expertise, so I've never dealt with him in an official capacity."

"Maybe I should have sent you down there to talk to him instead of me. He's still holding a grudge against me from our high school years." Adam's memory of my shortcomings was a little too long and his attitude retaliative. "He said I'm not nice like my father was. Can you believe it?"

Bryce laughed, the corners of his eyes crinkling. "From what I understand, none of the local government officials give out-of-town lawyers a break on anything."

"But I'm Hank's daughter. Working for his clients."

He shrugged. "Doesn't matter. You now have two black marks against you. Outsider and not nice." His chuckle hit a nerve.

I huffed. "No use worrying about it now. Friday's the day he'll give me his final answer."

At a little after noon, I stepped out of Bryce's office with a to-do list that would have been daunting to the winner of the Type-A workaholic personality contest.

"Hi, EJ." Dylan's voice echoed down the hall.

I turned, and he was heading toward me. Didn't Carol have control over clients who simply showed up without an appointment? But of course he probably assumed his "big" retainer and prominent position in his father's company meant he could interrupt my day at a moment's notice.

"I was in the area and stopped by to see if you were able to fast-track my permits yesterday." Hope in the form of a smile beamed across his face.

Although he had a somewhat nicer way about him

than Ron Briar and was an eleven on a ten-point gorgeousness scale, he was mistaken if he thought his dazzling white grin and flashing blue eyes would seduce me like the women beside him in that business magazine.

While I didn't mind gazing at that incredibly handsome countenance, I'd have to dash his optimism. "No. Not yet. I spoke to Adam Colton, the permit officer, and he said he'd let me know on Friday whether he'll issue the permits or make us apply for a variance. I'll advise you as soon as I hear." I tried to inject a bit of cheeriness into my voice, but I was drained from the morning's marathon meeting, not to mention the load of work hovering over me that I'd agreed to take on.

"I was hoping now that you're here, things would run more smoothly."

His initial pleasantness morphed into what I heard as criticism, and my blood boiled. I was seconds away from screeching that I'd only arrived yesterday and had a mountain of problems other than just his to deal with. So back off. Instead, I bit my lip, balled my fists, and said through gritted teeth, "Could you give me a moment, please?" Then I turned, went into my office, and closed the door. I gave myself props for not slamming it.

Inhaling deeply, I counted to ten. Then I did it again while walking in a circle. Two more times were necessary to diminish the angst in my gut.

After taking a sip of water from a bottle on my desk, I opened the door and was about to go to the reception area to talk to Dylan. But he was still standing in the hall where I'd left him.

Mr. *Business USA* was just as demanding as my

San Francisco clients, despite his presence in Wylder. Why had I thought the cases here would be simple and direct—almost a vacation from my normal workload?

Calling forth every bit of tact and pleasantness I had within, I spoke. "While I'm waiting to hear back, I plan to review your entire file and evaluate the unsigned contracts by the end of the day." My tone wasn't exactly cordial, but it was the best I could do under the circumstances. "As I said yesterday, I'll call you if I have any questions. But thank you for stopping by in case I needed anything."

I shouldn't really be angry with him. He was a typical prosperous business client who required my services and wanted everything done last week. My frustration came from the pressure he was putting on me along with the backlog of work that had piled up in the two short months since my father died. Fourteen days off to deal with it all was like getting twenty minutes to research an issue for the debate team competition. Insufficient, risky, and courting disaster. Adding to it all my mother's precarious position with regard to finances and a municipal official who held a grudge, I was close to the edge of the cliff.

He studied my face, perhaps searching for some clue as to what I was really thinking, but I hid my exasperation beneath a passive expression.

"Okay, then. Let me know when you hear."

"Of course." I watched him as he strode down the hallway, all long, lean male brimming with the self-assuredness that came from being the heir apparent to a multimillion-dollar redevelopment company. One who could have been on a catwalk in Paris or New York modeling those dark jeans and black pullover that fit him to perfection. An unexpected sigh escaped.

I'd better get my eyes off Mr. Addison's butt and put them on his unsigned contracts.

I returned to my office, opened the very large file labelled *Addison Real Estate*, and got to work. I didn't look up until it was dark outside and my eyes blurred.

****

I slipped out the front door and breathed in the cool, spring, evening air. The town was quiet, with most businesses locking their doors at six during the week.

My father's office was right next to the Wylder Hotel, a place I now knew intimately after reviewing the entire file including the architect's rendering. I stood before the front door, which held a sign—*Closed Temporarily for Renovations*. A dim light shone through the empty lobby, its faded green-velvet couches and linoleum-tiled floor proving its age. This hotel had seen better days.

When I was a child, this was the place where all my relative's weddings had been held. It's where my parents had thrown my high school graduation party. Now it was a sad, empty relic. A relic that Dylan aspired to turn into a jewel.

I startled when the front door opened.

Dylan emerged. "EJ, what are you doing here?"

"I was just leaving work. Heading back to my mom's. But first I decided to take a stroll around town to get the kinks out. I've been cooped up in my office for hours."

A look akin to sympathy played across his face. "Almost everything is closed."

"Yes. A little different than San Francisco." I took

in the spiral notebook he was carrying with various papers hanging out at intervals. "Were you coming up with more legal work?"

He chuckled. "No. I got the impression this afternoon you've had it with me."

Uh-oh. And here I'd thought my poker face had been on display. "No. That's not true. I'm sorry if that's the impression I gave. I've just been overwhelmed with everything there is to do." I sighed. "For some reason, I thought it would be easier. You know, a small-town law practice should have small-town legal issues."

"And it doesn't." His amused look at my erroneous theory struck a chord, and guilt over my prejudice swarmed through me.

"I've been biased living and working in San Francisco. Thinking that I'm counseling first-rate clients who have much more significant problems than those I'd experience if I came back to work with my dad. In the two days I've been here, I can see that the legal work, while on a smaller scale, is just as important."

"Good to hear. I wouldn't want you to minimize my needs." A grin accompanied his words, softening the barb.

Not likely with your constant hovering. "What have you been doing?" I nodded toward his notebook.

"Going over my list and second-guessing myself as to what to do first. This place is sure in need of a facelift."

Vulnerability clouded his magnificent eyes, and for a second, I thought maybe he wasn't so bad after all. "Well...I'll leave you to it. I'm sure I'll see you around." Hopefully, my words came out as affable rather than sarcastic, although he did seem to be constantly underfoot. Perhaps Adam was right. I needed to be nicer.

He cut into my musings. "Do you mind if I walk with you? I'm heading in the same direction."

"I don't mind." What else could I say that wouldn't sound less than Wylder friendly? We walked in silence for a few seconds.

"Did you review the contracts this afternoon?" Of course he would bring up business. Maybe I shouldn't have agreed to his company.

"Yes. There are some terms that should be negotiated, but for the most part, they're fine. I'll send you an email tomorrow with my comments, and you can let me know what you want to do."

His smile lit up the night. "That is the best news I've heard in months. Thank you, thank you, thank you."

His excitement boosted my mood. I hadn't realized how tired I was from my already long day and contemplating what would be waiting for me once I opened my laptop tonight.

"I'm glad I was able to get it done for you." It was that or lose a client that the firm badly needed. "Your plans look awfully ambitious. Replacing electrical wiring, all new plumbing, heating, and air conditioning, in addition to removing some walls."

He laughed. "I wish that was all. Once that's done, I'm having the entire place painted, re-carpeted, and decorated with new fixtures, furniture, and a huge chandelier, which will hang in the lobby."

"That sounds very expensive."

Of course, I was used to working on multimillion-dollar deals representing the purchaser or seller of high-end office buildings, retail stores, and hotels in San Francisco. The Wylder Hotel was much smaller than the thirty- to sixty-floor buildings I generally dealt with.

"It is for this area. Addison Redevelopment usually purchases and renovates buildings in bigger cities. Chicago is where the majority of our projects are located."

"Why Wylder? You could have at least chosen Cheyenne, the biggest city in Wyoming, instead of this small town." I glanced at him to analyze any telltale facial expression.

"I'm not crazy, if that's what you're thinking. A new theme park is going to be built outside of Wylder in the next few years, and once that happens, tourism will surge in this area. The Wylder Hotel will be ready to offer a quaint small-town experience to those coming from afar."

I pondered that bit of intel. "Very astute to research what's coming. But what if the theme park doesn't materialize?" I knew from my dealings in real estate that planning and zoning boards often denied ambitious developers who would change the landscape and the essence of the surrounding communities. Not everyone wanted a huge attraction in their backyard.

"If it doesn't get built, Wylder will still have a first-rate hotel. We'll just have to market it to a different audience." He stopped in front of the Vincent House. "I'm staying here." He paused, his mouth slightly ajar as if contemplating his next words. "Have you eaten dinner?"

"No. I didn't have a moment to run to the coffee shop and grab a sandwich. Hopefully, my mom will have saved me something." Although I wasn't at all sure that was the case, and now that he raised the issue, my stomach grumbled in protest.

"Would you like to have dinner with me at the restaurant here? I haven't eaten yet either and would love company."

While I could stare into those magnificent Caribbean Sea eyes for days on end, that wouldn't be productive. "Thank you, but I have to go through all my emails from my real job tonight and review a contract for one of my clients." I sighed, the hours of work ahead of me weighing me down.

"We can turn this dinner into a meeting. You can tell me the issues with the contracts so you don't have to write a long email tomorrow. And I can tell you what else I'll need your services for over the next few months. As I'm sure you saw in the file, we paid a large retainer to your father so we'd be well represented in this endeavor."

His words came with a smile, but it didn't erase the worry building in my gut over the future legal work he expected the firm to accomplish for him and his company. What would happen when I left in two weeks?

I swallowed my dread. "Okay. I guess you better lay it all out there."

He took my elbow as we walked up the steps toward the restaurant. His warm hand sent interesting flashes up my arm and to my core—a déjà vu from yesterday and more than a little disturbing that the touch of his hand could wreak such havoc within.

Yet it was so much better than the lump of anxiety those flashes had miraculously disintegrated.

Chapter Five
Dylan

I congratulated myself for convincing EJ to have dinner with me. The better understanding I had of her future goals, the better I'd be able to determine if we could work together. I needed to know that she'd be totally with me on this venture—like her dad had been. I didn't agree with my father's advice to hire an out-of-town firm with no ties to the community. But if EJ couldn't commit to representing me for the duration, I just might have to go that route.

Of course I didn't want to turn the entire dinner into a business meeting. I'd keep that portion of our evening together short and hopefully get to know some personal facts about the beautiful woman sharing a meal with me. Something about her stuck with me long after our meetings in her office and despite her frustration with me. I needed to explore that rush of pleasure that swam through my blood anytime we touched.

We sat at a table for two next to the window, and EJ glanced across the street. "I see the drug store has a new owner. Evans Apothecary. I wonder if Beth Evans bought the place. I think she went to college to become a pharmacist."

If small talk was the way to start, then so be it. "I've been in there dozens of times, but I only see the teens who work behind the counter. I haven't met the pharmacist."

Other than the electricians, plumbers, and carpenters that Hank had recommended I consider for the renovation, I hadn't met any other business owners in the time I'd spent in Wylder. Although it seemed like a friendly town, my determination to make this project a success kept my head down and my mind focused on the project at hand—except for the staff at the Vincent House, my home away from home.

Claire, the weeknight waitress, approached our table with a smile. "Hello, Dylan."

I'd eaten in here so often over the past few months I knew all the waitresses and bartenders.

Then she turned to EJ, and recognition dawned. "Hi, Emma Jane."

"Claire, it's nice to see you again." EJ returned Claire's smile before including me in the conversation. "Claire's older sister Jenna and I went to high school together. We became good friends in Mrs. Robinson's chemistry class since I didn't have a clue what was going on. Science was not my forte."

"I'm sure she'd love to see you. What brings you to town?"

"I'm helping my father's associate, Bryce, for a little while with the firm's clients."

EJ's gaze caught mine for a mere second, leaving me wondering what she was hiding behind that quick look. Although, if truth be told, I wouldn't mind trapping that gaze along with her full lips under mine. And why stop there? That body looked fine, even hidden under a business suit.

Claire broke through my steamy thoughts. "Bryce

is a nice guy. He comes in for lunch sometimes." She lowered her voice and directed her statement to EJ. "Put in a good word for me if you get a chance. I'd love to get to know him better." Her face reddened with her request.

EJ brushed her long caramel hair over her shoulder and smiled back. "Will do."

After Claire left us to peruse the menu, I put mine aside. "I know this menu by heart."

"How long have you been in Wylder?"

"Off and on since January, so going on five months."

"Then you must have met a lot of people in town by now."

"Not really. When I'm here, I pretty much keep to myself. Although I do know Claire since I eat in this restaurant all the time. Not well enough apparently for her to ask me to put in a good word for her with Bryce, even though she knows I spend a lot of time at your father's office."

"That's because you don't seem like the small-town, friendly type." Her inky eyes, more sapphire tonight in the overhead light, flashed with mischief, and a grin appeared on her luscious mouth.

"What do you mean? I'm friendly."

She bit her lip, drawing yet more attention to her mouth. "Small-town friendly is different. You're civil. But you're no-nonsense. Unapproachable. And very demanding. You dress like a rich business owner, which you are, but it sends the wrong message. Even though you think you're dressing down, your jeans are probably dry cleaned and your boots are polished Italian leather. The men around here wear flannel shirts, worn-out denims, cowboy boots. Have you noticed that you don't fit in?" Her laugh tickled my heart.

"Why do you fit in? You have on a designer suit, silk blouse, high heels. A big-city outfit if I've ever seen one." But of course, I loved that she stuck out like an emerald among sea glass.

"I have my lawyer uniform on. And I grew up here. People know me, despite my clothes. I could wear casual pants and a sweater to work while I'm here, but it doesn't send the right message. I definitely do not have to wear a suit. That would only be required if I were going to court. Or meeting with an out-of-town city client. Which I have been."

I felt my smile bloom. "So you're dressing to impress me?"

"No. Most definitely not." Her response held the hint of a bite despite her teasing demeanor. "Today is only my second day here. Yesterday I had no idea what or whom I was going to face."

I pushed the envelope. "You did today."

"You may recall that you showed up without an appointment. And tonight was a mere coincidence." A shadow crossed her face, and her voice softened. "My father dressed in a suit every day, even though it wasn't necessary. I was channeling his spirit." Sadness clouded those beautiful mercurial eyes. "Plus, my wardrobe changed when I moved to San Francisco."

Frankly, I didn't care what she wore. Designer duds, jeans, lacy underwear. Nothing. I smiled to myself at the direction my mind was veering. *Interesting.* "You seem very at ease here in Wylder. Why'd you leave? Why San Francisco?"

She stared out the window as if rewinding to her

past. "When you grow up in a small town like this, every person, every event, ever storefront and street brings back memories. Some good. Some bad." She lowered her lids, and dark lashes fanned over high cheekbones as her teeth worried her bottom lip. "Let's just say I couldn't wait to leave Wylder behind. I went to college at UC Berkley, then Stanford Law School." A shadow darkened those magnificent cobalt eyes, turning them indigo.

I hadn't meant to take her to a negative place in her vault of memories. My goal was to have a nice, relaxing dinner, get to know her a little—see if that spark she generated in me was something to follow up on—and work in some business. Thankfully, Claire appeared and took our order, allowing us to recalibrate.

EJ changed the subject first. "Would you like to discuss the contracts now?"

Since that's what got her to have dinner with me, I should acquiesce, but I veered off. "I'd prefer to discuss your game plan for Friday if the permit officer doesn't issue the permits. And filing an application for a variance is not the answer I want to hear."

"Your demanding, unapproachable, no-nonsense self is shining through. Are you sure you don't want to rephrase?" The grin inching over her lips, as her playful words counseled me to reconsider, dismantled my serious aura.

I felt my lips twitch as I reframed my sentence. "Perhaps you could contemplate a Plan B which does not require a variance?"

Her laughter squeezed my heart.

"So much better. But I could tell you what Plan B is right now. Forget about the additional storage space.

You'll get the permits right away and can start your renovation tomorrow. Once the municipality sees the great things you're doing for the town with a first-rate hotel, I don't think they would deny your request at a later date."

"Absolutely not." My tone shifted from conversational to steely, underscoring her insight that I was demanding and no-nonsense. I needed to tone it down a notch or ten. "If I want a five-star restaurant to bring people in, I need a spacious kitchen. No top chef would want to work in the poorly designed space as it stands. All the construction must be done at once. You know the costs will double if I wait. It's built into the renovations already. There is no way I would walk away from my original plan."

I knew my stance was intractable and my delivery unfriendly, just as she'd accused me of being, but she needed to know that as my lawyer, she had to buy into my plan.

She studied me with an unsettling gaze, as if to gauge whether she could soften my position. "That's fine. If we don't get the permits on Friday, I'll file an application for a variance and request an expedited meeting of the planning board."

Her cool and calm response in the face of my obstinate mandate made my heart trip over itself. She was a consummate professional who didn't let a challenging client ruffle her beautiful feathers.

I felt the need to explain my mulish position. "I'm sorry if I sound so headstrong. My father is breathing down my neck to get this renovation moving. If I don't, he intends to pull out."

"You mean abandon the project?" Shock flitted

across her face.

"Yes. We'd sell the hotel, even if at a loss, to stop future bigger losses. I don't want that to happen, which is why I'm pushing so hard." I spared her the fear that Addison Redevelopment might end up retaining other counsel if my father got his wish. EJ had enough on her plate right now without fretting over one of the firm's major clients abandoning ship.

Her initial shock morphed into worry lines marring her forehead. "That would be devastating to the town. The renovated hotel would surely bring more life to Wylder. If you leave, who knows if anyone else would buy it soon."

Obviously, she still cared deeply about her hometown, despite the fact she'd deserted it for San Francisco. Maybe she was secretly contemplating a move back even though she still talked about her job on the West Coast.

If I could do anything to help her with that decision, I wanted to know. In the space of a half hour, I was becoming mesmerized, not only with her eyes, but with her psyche. She was smart, well spoken, calm…and not to mention…beautiful.

What was happening? I hadn't felt the heat of a sexual connection in a while—not since I'd first started dating Lucia, my former fiancée.

But that had been over now for seven months, and the excitement in our relationship had ended long before that. While I was extremely attracted to powerful women, Lucia, the CFO of a major construction company, was cut from the same cloth as my father— going after the megadeals that would line their pockets with no regard for the people they'd be affecting. EJ seemed different. But only time would tell.

Our dinner arrived, and I steered clear of further business discussions. I wanted to know everything I could about the intelligent and charming woman before me.

"Your father said you stayed in California longer than he'd anticipated. What kept you there?"

She cut into her chicken marsala, her facial expression composed but her jaw tense. "I was learning an incredible amount from my boss and mentor at the firm, and it was exciting to work on multimillion-dollar deals. There are so many moving parts as well as governmental agencies to navigate. The transactions I'm involved in take a year or more to finalize, and the satisfaction in closing such complicated deals far exceeded my assumptions of what small-town legal work would entail." She took a sip of her wine and gazed out the window, worlds away from San Francisco. "I'm also the coach of the moot court team at Berkeley. That position is something of a personal triumph. It means a lot to me."

Her reasoning all made sense, but I couldn't help wondering if there was more to it. I took a bite of my steak, wrestling with myself as to whether to ask the nagging question on my mind. So I went for it. "Do you have a boyfriend back there waiting for you?" Best to know what I'd be dealing with up front.

A pretty blush rose up on her cheeks. "I did. But we broke up before Christmas." She shrugged as if to say no big deal. "What about you? What's with all the women you were photographed with for that *Business USA* article?"

I chuckled, but embarrassment streamed through

my pores. "The magazine had me show up at different places to take photos, and each time they directed me to do something with a different model they'd hired. There were a lot more people around, so I assumed we were merely part of a fun-loving crowd. I didn't know they were going to edit the photos to make it look like I was with the woman of the week. For some reason, the editor at the magazine wanted to characterize me as a philanderer. Which I am not."

Her gaze studied me as if to determine the truth of my words. But what else could I say? She'd make up her own mind about me once she got to know me better.

I brought the conversation back to her. "Would you have come back to work with your dad this year if he had lived?"

She dabbed at her mouth with her napkin. "When he died in March, that vision died with him. I don't want to speculate about what I would have done, because it doesn't matter anymore. Now I'll probably stay in San Francisco indefinitely and do my thing."

"You don't want to eventually take over the firm?" A sudden chill breezed through my veins at the possibility I might never see her again after these few weeks.

"Probably not." A frown creased her brow. "Why?"

She was right to ask that question. Why would I care whether she returned to her hometown? Unless I was selfish enough to want her legal skills involved in representing me. Or if I was interested in pursuing something with her. But I couldn't go there. I'd met her only yesterday. Yet something about her pulled me in, forming a connection. She was a warrior and a peacemaker at the same time—taking charge and pushing back at my demands while smoothing my feathers, refusing to get ruffled herself. She used tact and humor to control me. No one had ever accused me of being demanding and unapproachable. At least not to my face. But with her I was able to laugh while being castigated.

"Can I get either of you anything else right now?" Claire yanked me out of my thoughts and saved me from having to answer EJ's question.

"No, thank you. EJ, do you need anything?"

She shook her head and gave Claire a wan smile. Had she too been locked in an internal debate about how much to share?

"I did want to come back one day." Her answer rang strong, determined. "I wanted to work with my dad. I just needed more time." She put her fork down, staring at the food before her. "Now it will never happen."

"If you took over the firm, you'd be continuing his legacy. Perpetuating it through you."

She blinked. "Is that what you're doing by working with your father? Are you preparing to take over the company at some point in the future?"

"I'm sure that's my father's plan. And I suppose it's mine too. He's been slowly giving me non-voting shares in the company." I chuckled to myself. "Voting shares would give me too much power, and I don't have the same vision as my father. We have different philosophies about certain projects, and he doesn't want to hear anything that doesn't jive with his. I started looking for properties out here to prove that we should have a small-town acquisition division. It's something

I've been passionate about since I renovated my grandparents' bed and breakfast. I saw what it did for the community. That one renovation elevated the town, encouraged other growth, and turned it from a sleepy village into a destination, bringing in business and money to the townspeople." I sounded like I was stumping for votes from my audience of one.

"Your father must be proud of you for following through on your concept."

I inhaled a frustrated breath. "My father is only interested in big developments in big cities. He's more about making tons of money and basks in the prestige that comes with flashy projects. He believes small-town renovations are a waste of time. I want to prove him wrong with this venture."

Her face softened with my candid admission. "While I knew this project was important to you from a business perspective, now I can see there's a personal stake as well."

"It's going to be impossible to convince him my idea is solid if I don't get this hotel up and running soon. As I told you, he would have no qualms about selling it, even if it's at a loss, unless things start moving. I know this type of work can be profitable. Not only for us, but for the community we're working in. If I fail at this project, I won't get another chance."

Her eyebrow arched. "Wow. He's tough."

The anxiety I'd been living with since the day Hank Hampton died attacked me with a vengeance. "That's why I've been so relentless in stopping by the office every day to find out about the status of those permits—pushing Bryce to use whatever connections he has to drive the application through. When he finally did make a few calls, it resulted with the letter stating that I needed a variance. If you can't work your magic on the person in charge, the project will be dead."

Sympathy shadowed her eyes. And perhaps a little dread that she was the catalyst that could make or break me. She clearly understood the dilemma I was in. She probably faced similar problems with her San Francisco clients all the time.

Her hand inched across the table to mine, and she covered it with what was probably meant to be a comforting pat. I turned my wrist, and my fingers stroked her palm. It was cool and warm at the same time, and the now familiar electricity she generated through our simple touch was magnetic. I thought I saw a shiver course through her body as she pulled her hand away.

"I should get going." Her voice was husky, sexy. "I still have work to do once I get home, and I have an early meeting with an accountant tomorrow morning." She turned to look for Claire. "We need to get the check."

She avoided my eyes, clearly trying to sever our connection.

"The tab is covered. I have all my meals here billed to the room." I stood, disappointment over her abrupt departure filling every space inside me. "I'll walk you back to your car."

"Thank you. For the meal and the offer to walk me back, but that's not necessary. It was nice to get to know a little more about your business." Her tone had gone from casual to formal.

Not good on any level. My discussion about the hotel had turned our getting-to-know-you conversation into a plea for help, and while it generated a private moment of empathy, my intimacy scared her off. I'd have to work harder at getting her to let her guard down.

Or I'd lose the possibility of fanning this electrifying desire into a flame even before my father pulled the plug.

Chapter Six
Emma Jane

What was I doing reaching across the table to touch him? If that was my first thought of the morning immediately after hitting the snooze button on my alarm, I was in big trouble. I squeezed my eyes shut as if to erase the picture implanted in my brain, but I couldn't dislodge it. Those intense blue eyes had connected with mine as his fingers stroked the palm of my hand. Even now thrills coursed up my arm, and shivers ran through my blood.

I eased out of bed, all the while trying to convince myself it meant nothing. I'd been consoling a client over the difficulties he had with his father, and he'd accepted my sympathy.

But I had never done anything remotely close to comforting a client. Sure, I was reassuring and encouraging in the face of obstacles, but I had never let my professional guard down as I had last night. What was it with Dylan Addison?

I didn't have time to analyze it, nor did I want to. It was a one-time thing that would never happen again. End of story.

I turned on the coffee maker, washed my face, and brushed my teeth before settling in at the table, which now served as my desk. I'd have a few hours to work on my files before my ten-o'clock meeting.

After parking behind the law office, I walked the few blocks to my destination, needing to clear my head of the current repetitious questions spinning out of control—would I be able to fast-track Dylan's permits before his father scrapped the project—and more personally, would I find a buyer for my father's practice before it went under?

I inhaled the fresh Wyoming air while enjoying a bit of exercise, but much too soon I entered the accounting office of Emerson and Roberts. I'd learned that Sam Emerson had done the law firm's taxes as well as my parents' personal returns for years.

"It's so nice to see you again, EJ."

Sam held out his hand, and I shook it, noticing the casual business clothes he wore. I really needed to tone it down a bit myself. Bryce and I appeared to be the only people in town who wore suits.

"Thank you for squeezing me in on such short notice."

He offered me coffee, which I gladly accepted and took a seat in his office across from him.

"My purpose in meeting with you is for a confidential inquiry."

His salt-and-pepper brows inched up. "What is it?"

"Do you know of any lawyers in the area who may be interested in buying my father's practice?"

He steepled his fingers under his chin. "I can't say that question is a surprise, but I thought perhaps you'd consider taking over."

"No, definitely not." I shook my head to underscore my words. "I came home for two weeks at my mom's request to figure out what to do about the business. It appears that Bryce can't handle the caseload, and he doesn't know of any lawyer with my father's capabilities who is looking for a job. Our only choice is to sell the practice." I ignored the lariat that strangled my heart. "Perhaps you could help us find a buyer?"

Sam studied me with uncompromising eyes. "That's not your only choice."

"What else is there?"

"You could change your mind and take over."

Why were those words dropped so casually by others? As if I didn't have a job, a life, a home in California. I had friends whom I hiked with and met for happy hour on Fridays. I was on a recreational volleyball team that played on Wednesdays. I had a great career at a highly respected law firm with a promise of partnership in the not-too-distant future. And I no longer had Ashley or my dad to practice law with.

"As I said before, that's not my intent. So in keeping with the only valid option, we'll need someone to assess the business's worth before selling. I'm starting with you. Do you or any of your colleagues evaluate businesses? If not, perhaps you can direct me to the right consultants."

His mouth twitched as he sat back in his big leather chair and rocked. "My partner, Dave Roberts, does business evaluations, and I'm sure he could value the business with your help. With regard to a purchaser, I don't know of any lawyers in town who are actively looking to take over a practice, but I can make some discreet inquiries. In and out of town."

The way he measured his words, along with his calm, skillful demeanor, erased the tension I'd been carrying on my shoulders. So comforting. I exhaled some of the pent-up stress buried deep in my core. "That would be great. I'd be so appreciative of your help. My mom too."

"You both have been dealt quite a blow. No one expected your father to pass. He was so young and vibrant, one of the pillars of this town. I miss him a lot."

I bit my lip and stared at my knuckles, forcing those pesky tears to stay put. "Do you want me to sign an engagement letter for the business evaluation?" Getting down to the matter at hand should work effectively to dodge my emotions. "How much is your retainer?"

"No need for a retainer. We'll bill you for Dave's time on an hourly basis, with a courtesy discount of course. With regard to the other issue, I'd be more than happy to help you free of charge. I want to see the firm that your father built continue to thrive. We owe it to him."

My throat ached, along with my heart. All I could do was nod.

I stood to go.

"I'll be in touch with my findings." He came around his desk, and this time, instead of shaking my hand, he placed his arm around my shoulders and gave me a comforting squeeze. "Tell your mom I said hello."

"Will do." I gave him a grateful smile and left.

Standing on the sidewalk, I felt my emotions ram into each other. I had dozens of files to work on back at the office, but I needed a mental break. Without further thought, I walked to Amber's Boutique. The tiny bell over the door tinkled at my entrance.

The owner looked up from arranging colorful scarves, a smile for a customer etched on her mouth. "EJ!" she squealed. "What are you doing here?" A silk scarf fluttered to the floor.

Amber, one of my dear friends since first grade, had opened this boutique a few years back, and anytime I was in town, I stopped by to gossip and shop.

Just seeing her buoyed my spirits, and I strode over to hug her. "I'm here to help out at the law firm for two weeks." The burden I thought I'd left with Sam reappeared. "There's so much to do to get things under control that two weeks will never be enough. But that's all my boss would give me."

She took my hands and squeezed them. "I know what will lift your mood. Some shopping. Come over here." She drew me to a rack of pastel-hued dresses. "These are just in for spring. Aren't they gorgeous?" She lifted a hanger from the bar and held up a dress. "You would look amazing in this."

I fingered the smooth material. "It is beautiful. But I don't have time."

"Yes, you do." She drew me toward a dressing room and pushed me in. "I'll bring over some others."

I laughed. It felt good to have someone else take control. I'd just try on a few and be on my way. As I changed into the first dress, Amber segued into her next best trait—town gossip.

"Did you hear that a big developer from Chicago bought the Wylder Hotel and intends to renovate it?"

I smiled to myself. "I did."

"Wait until you meet him. His name is Dylan Addison, and he's gorgeous. And single." She pushed three more outfits through the fitting-room curtain. "Do you have the first dress on yet? Come on out. I want to see it."

I stepped out of the cubicle garbed in a pink, flowery wrap dress, so different from the tailored suit I'd just removed.

"I love it on you," gushed Amber. "It's so feminine and romantic. You should wear that when you meet Dylan."

"You seem to have this all planned out. You know his name. His occupation. And that he's single. Did you add a matchmaking business to your boutique?" I looked at my reflection in the mirror and spun to see the back. "This is really pretty. But do you see me wearing flowers?" My scrunched face scowled back at me.

She laughed. "I haven't seen you in a floral print since middle school, but that doesn't mean you shouldn't wear one. It's a nice change from navy, black, and gray, don't you think?"

I had to agree. I felt light and airy and fairy-like.

"Try on the rest before you decide." She shooed me back to the dressing room.

"You're very bossy today."

"You don't have much time, and I want to see how these dresses look on a real person. You're the perfect model."

I did as I was told and emerged in a sky-blue and yellow geometric print dress with a matching belt. "This is more like something I would wear."

"It is, and it fits perfectly. You should get both. I'm sure you'll have more than one date with Mr. Addison once he meets you."

"What makes you think I haven't met him?" I smirked.

Her smile exploded. "Did you? Isn't he so handsome?" She was practically jumping up and down.

"I did, and he is." I felt my own smile grow. "He's a client of the firm. I'm working with him to get the permits he needs to start renovations."

"That's perfect. Then you'll need more than two outfits if you'll be here for two weeks. You can't wear your stuffy suits to dinner. You shouldn't even wear them to the office. No one dresses like that around here." She disappeared into the store and came back with assorted casual pants and tops to add to the dresses I'd already chosen. "You'll need something for the Spring Festival. It's a week from Saturday. You'll still be here, right?"

"Oh my God. Yes. How could I forget! I love that festival." There was one celebration or another almost every month, a bit much for the townspeople who participated, as well as for the municipal budget, according to my mom. But Wylder loved its festivals. "With everything else going on, it hadn't even crossed my mind. I'm surprised my mom didn't mention it. Maybe she's not involved this year."

"Oh, your mom is involved. She's the co-chair with Beth Conti." Amber's perpetually happy aura turned grim. "I know they're having a hard time getting funding from the municipality for certain events. Supposedly, there's not enough money in the budget this year."

"That's too bad."

"I know. Maybe you can get your new client to be a sponsor. It might help him move from an outsider to a semi-local with at least one foot on the inside."

I chuckled. "Is he that much of an outcast? He's

been around since January."

"Off and on. He goes back and forth to Chicago. When he is here, he keeps to himself. I haven't seen him at the Five Star Saloon on weekends, and really, that's the only place to go on a Friday or Saturday night. He wasn't at the spring dance." She shrugged. "I know he's new to town and his company is headquartered in Chicago, but if he wants the locals to give him business when he opens, he should do a little more to fit in."

She was right. The residents in small towns like Wylder looked out for their own. The business owners helped each other by supporting the surrounding shops. They used the catering services from the town restaurants for special occasions and bought everything from groceries, medicines, clothing, and gifts from stores within a three-mile radius.

"Have you met Dylan personally?" I asked.

"No. Our paths haven't crossed."

"Well, maybe you should change that. As you said, he's handsome and single. Why aren't you stepping up to the plate?"

Amber and her most recent boyfriend had broken up after five years together. I'd thought he was the one for her, but he didn't want to settle in Wylder, and Amber had no intention of moving to a bigger city. End of relationship.

A telling blush rose to her cheeks. "I'm interested in someone else."

"Do tell." We generally shared the details of our ill-fated relationships, hoping the next would be the winner. And by the looks of her smile and fluttering hands, she was smitten.

"You have to get back to work, and I have a new shipment coming in soon. Why don't we get together for a drink some night while you're in town? I'll bring you up to date."

"You got it. Let me know what works for you."

I stood at the register as she entered my purchases—more than I'd intended—bantering about the new owner of the bakery and his to-die-for cinnamon caramel muffins, the mailman who continually brought her the neighbor's mail even though she'd told him umpteen times that Mrs. Dalton did not live with her, and the new policy at the high school that banned kids from walking into town during lunch or study breaks.

As I handed over my credit card, I couldn't help but wonder whether I would wear any of these new outfits while having dinner with Dylan. This morning I had convinced myself to stay away from any personal interactions and only discuss business either over the phone or in the office. But a curious little fantasy was still buzzing around, teasing my carnal cravings.

Of course, if I couldn't convince Adam to issue those permits without a variance, all would be lost, and I highly doubted we'd be breaking bread together.

****

As I worked on file after file, getting them organized and determining the next steps to be taken, my conversation with Amber was never far from my mind. Dylan had to become a part of this community— and fast. If he did, maybe others would stand behind him, and Adam or, God forbid, the planning board, if necessary, would issue those permits immediately. Maybe he could do something concrete for the Spring

Festival that would show the townspeople he was one of them.

I picked up the phone. "Hi, Dylan. Are you free for dinner tonight? I want to discuss something with you." Had my mouth not been involved in the discussions with my head? What happened with meeting him at the office?

"What a nice invitation." His tone suggested a smile. "No small talk. Just a direct request. I like that."

I laughed. "I'm not asking you out on a date. I'm calling you as your lawyer. And since you're paying me by the minute, I'm guessing you don't want me to waste time on banal pleasantries."

"So dinner's on the clock?" Disappointment trailed through the line.

"I don't intend to bill you, so no. I have an idea that I want to explore with you." One that apparently couldn't be explored by phone or email or in the office with Carol right outside my door. I clunked my forehead with my palm.

"That sounds interesting. What time and where?"

"Does six work at the Five Star Saloon? It's on the corner of Sidewinder Lane and Old Cheyenne Road."

My choice of venue was twofold. Foremost, there would be no private moments between us like there had been last night at dinner. Secondly, I intended to introduce him to some of the locals—those who did not frequent the more upscale Vincent House Restaurant.

"Slumming it, are we? Or do you prefer raucous pubs to quieter spaces?"

His chuckle led me to believe he knew I didn't want to hit replay on my wandering hand reaching over to touch his.

"I'd prefer to stay in the town center, and the Five Star is a happening place. Plus, they have great burgers."

"Okay. The Five Star it is. See you at six."

I hung up and immediately called my mother. "You didn't tell me you were co-chairing the Spring Festival."

"You have so much on your plate, dear. I didn't want to distract you."

"I saw Amber this morning, and she said the municipality is cutting the funding. What specifically do you need?"

"Well…the local businesses all have booths as usual, which is covering the food and drinks. But we are working on the setup for the various games. We not only need physical manpower, but the funds to rent the booths. And I'm afraid we're not going to have fireworks this year."

"But fireworks are the crowning jewel to the entire day."

"I know." My mom's sigh echoed through the line.

"Do you have a list of everything you need along with estimates of costs?"

"Of course. I've been going to all the businesses in town to request monetary donations to cover what we still need. I also created a sponsorship form with specifics."

"Can you drop it by before six tonight?"

"Oh, honey. You can't take this on too."

I chuckled. "Don't worry, Mom. I'm not. I have one possible sponsor who I'll be speaking to later. Don't get your hopes up, but he may be able to help."

I blew out a breath. And it might just help him too.

Chapter Seven
Dylan

I walked into the Five Star Saloon a little before six, my eyes adjusting to the dim atmosphere. A throwback to earlier days, the walls were paneled in rough-cut pine and decorated with animal heads—a few with antlers. The bar's polished mahogany gleamed under strategically placed ceiling lights, and a brass footrail ran around the base. This place probably hadn't changed much since the late eighteen hundreds.

Except for the clientele, which now included women. Even so, the dress was decidedly rancher, with dozens of flannel shirts, dusty jeans, mud-caked boots, and cowboy hats.

I was about to ask for a booth in the back, away from the bar, when EJ arrived—a sparkling diamond among iron ore. A geometric form-fitting dress had replaced her tailored suit, and her lush golden-brown hair was spun into a loose bun at the crown of her head with cascading wisps falling around that beautiful face. Dark-blue eyes flashed with a hint of sapphire, picking up one of the colors in her dress.

"Hi." Her brilliant smile did funny things to my insides.

"I was just about to grab a booth in the back." At least there we wouldn't be the center of attention.

She steered me to one across from the bar. "This

one is better." She sat facing the door.

I slid in across from her. "Are you orchestrating something?" I couldn't control my grin.

"I have the impression you don't know many people in town. That has to change."

Just then the bartender yelled over. "EJ, what can I get you?"

"I'll let you know in a minute, Chad," she called back.

I couldn't help my eyebrow lift. "No waitress here?"

"Sometimes." She shrugged. "It depends on the day. And sometimes it depends if she bothers to show up. Wanda has been working here since I was a kid. I'm not sure why she hasn't retired yet since she seemed old then, but I guess it keeps her going. So what would you like to drink?"

"I could walk up to the bar to order."

She chuckled. "Chad will ignore you. I assume this is the first time you've been here since you're looking around like it's a novelty."

"I tend to stick to the restaurant at the hotel. I feel comfortable there. Welcome may be a better word, but I'm not a hundred percent sure it's true." Although I'd been in town off and on for months, I hadn't made any friends, other than Hank.

"The time has come to pull you out of your comfort zone. If you want to fit in with the locals, you're going to have to start associating with them."

Apparently giving up on me to decide on a drink, she called over to the bartender. "Chad, we'll have two Snake River Pale Ales."

"I'm not a big beer drinker."

Her gaze targeted mine as if to say what we ordered was not the point of this outing.

I held up both hands to concede.

Chad came around the bar with our beers and clunked them on the table. "What brings you to town, EJ?"

"I'm helping out at my dad's firm for two—for a little while."

"Great. This town could use another Hampton attorney."

Surprise crinkled her brow, although I didn't know the reason.

"I want to introduce you to Dylan Addison. He bought the Wylder Hotel and is going to renovate it. Dylan, this is Chad Wilson, the owner of this establishment."

I shook Chad's hand as the man studied me.

"I heard that a bigwig from Chicago bought the hotel. Are you going to turn it into some glitzy, hoity-toity resort?" Disdain darkened his face.

So that was the fear. "No, not at all. I'm simply giving it a little facelift since it's slightly out of date." More than slightly, but I didn't want to set Chad off with any negativity.

I hoped the bartender slash owner would return to his station, but EJ continued to engage with him.

"Remember how nice the hotel was when we were growing up? The senior prom was held there for years. Dylan plans to bring it back to its former glory. In addition to bringing more tourists to our area, it will be nice to have a big party space in town again, don't you think? As well as another restaurant option for breakfast and lunch."

"I hope it doesn't interfere with business here," he groused.

She soothed his feathers. "This place has a huge clientele and a great following. The hotel restaurant will cater more to tourists and business people. There's nothing to worry about, Chad." She gifted him with a smile that I would have much preferred she direct at me, but she was clearly trying to help me out with one of the local business owners.

I joined my cause. "EJ told me this is the place to come for the best burgers in town."

"Yep. It's also the top karaoke venue. Stick around. It starts at eight tonight." Chad clapped me on the back, not exactly a friendly move. "I'll put in your order for two burgers."

Without asking for our specific requests, he sauntered back to the bar and got busy.

I let out the breath I hadn't known I was holding. "I'm not sure I made a friend."

EJ took a sip of her beer. "It may take some time, but you'll win him over. If you start coming here at least once a week. Even if it's just to have a quick drink at the bar or a sandwich at lunchtime. Get to know him, as well as the customers." She nodded toward the bar at the few-dozen townspeople who all seemed like best friends. "You need to do this with all the businesses around town. What have you been doing for the past five months?" Her brow scrunched as she waited for my sorry excuse.

I would have grinned in an attempt to soften her underlying admonishment, but she might have then assumed I wasn't taking her advice seriously. I cleared my throat. "I have projects in Chicago that I've continued to work on. When I'm in town, I've been dealing with contractors, getting estimates. The usual."

"At least you're using local tradespeople for the hotel."

She would know that since she'd reviewed the contracts.

"Was introducing me to Chad your sole purpose in asking me to meet you here?" I had hoped it was because she was as intrigued with me as I was with her. The heat in her eyes when I stroked her palm last night couldn't have been an illusion.

"Not my sole purpose." Her sly smile gave me hope. "The Spring Festival is in nine days. You may have seen the signs around town."

All hope was dashed with this turn in the conversation. I had seen the signs, but it wasn't something I put in my calendar. Although perhaps I should, to assure I wouldn't get stuck in traffic if I wanted to get out of town that day. "And?" There had to be more.

"The town's budget is tight this year, and they can't afford fireworks. That's a big draw, so disappointment is running high. There are a few other things that need funding." She opened her purse and withdrew a folded piece of paper. "My mom is co-chair of the event, and these are their current needs."

I took the paper and scanned a host of sponsorship opportunities along with the estimated cost next to each. The most expensive by far was the fireworks. I searched her face. "Are you asking me for a donation? I can certainly write a check to contribute."

"Does your father's company support community festivities?"

Oh, so this was where she was going. "Sometimes."

"I know you said he wasn't quite on board with the purchase of the hotel, but you also seemed fairly certain he'd come around. If Addison Redevelopment gave a significant donation toward the fireworks, I could use that information to help move your permit applications along. These types of things aren't forgotten, so it may be beneficial to both you and your father in the future."

I knew EJ was a savvy business attorney, but I hadn't expected her to come right out and suggest something awfully close to a bribe. I raised my brow. "Is that how things get done in Wylder?"

Her laugh lightened my heart. "That's how things get done everywhere. We're simply more transparent in Wylder. Why beat around the bush when you can just come out and say it?"

I glanced at the paper I still held. "The price is pretty steep for not being assured I'll have no problem getting my permits."

"I agree. And I'm glad you recognize that any donation is not a guarantee. But financial help with the festival is part of the overall plan to ingratiate yourself with this community. Something you haven't done yet. It's a great opportunity to let the townspeople know who you are and that you intend to participate—not just swoop in, buy a hotel, renovate it, and leave. That's not your plan, is it?"

"No. I would like to work on more projects in the area once I get the hotel up and running. I've been scouting other locations for possible development deals once the hotel takes off. Assuming I can convince my father this is the way to go."

"You told me why you chose Wylder instead of Cheyenne, but I'm still confused over how you ended up in Wyoming. It's not like we're in your neighborhood. We're a thousand miles away from Chicago."

"Wyoming has had a pull on me for years. My grandparents lived in a small town near Laramie. My two brothers and I would visit them every summer for a few weeks. We'd go fishing and hiking and swimming. It was the best part of the summer—getting away from the city and exploring our freedom in the woods. I loved it." I felt my smile start from within. "Although I lived in the city my entire life, it was those summers that had me dreaming of a different path. One that was more laid-back, more friendly, less cutthroat."

"Why didn't you go back to your grandparents' town to look for a project?"

"I wanted to be closer to the capital city. Since Wylder is near Cheyenne, it was more logical."

She nodded her acceptance of my explanation. "Have you taken advantage of the hiking trails and lakes in this area?"

"I have. On weekends, I disappear. I've hiked several times on the Sidewinder Trail and canoed on the Medicine Bow River. It's so peaceful. I tried my hand at fishing in Horseshoe Lake, but it's not as much fun as I thought it was as a kid. A little too sedate for me."

Our burgers arrived, thick and juicy and huge. "Thanks, Chad." I made sure to engage with him as instructed. "This looks and smells amazing. I may have to come in here more often."

EJ turned to Chad. "You're having your booth at the Spring Festival, right?"

"Wouldn't miss it for the world. I understand the town is scaling back, though, this year. And can you believe we're not having fireworks? That's sacrilegious."

She found my shin with the toe of her shoe.

"EJ was just telling me the same thing." I commiserated with Chad. "I'm going to reach out to my CEO tonight to see if we can help turn this around."

He beamed. "That would be terrific if you could sponsor them. The town would surely be grateful."

"I can't make any promises, but I'll do my best." My father would resist at first, but I had a few potential projects in the area for him to consider, which might loosen the money from the company's community trust.

When Chad left us to eat, EJ grinned. "If you get the money, make sure you come in here tomorrow and tell Chad while you're having a drink at the bar. He'll tell every customer who comes in after that."

"It's good to have you on my side." I sought out her gaze, connecting through those magnificent navy orbs. She awarded me with a dazzling smile.

"It's the least I could do after you've hung in there for the past two months following my dad's death. I really appreciate your loyalty to the firm."

I did want to remain with the firm, especially now that she was working on my case. Although she wasn't a current Wylder resident, she still fit in. People knew her and respected her, and she understood how to accomplish something in this town. Just like Hank. I was getting the added benefit of spending time with this intelligent, confident woman who sparked something inside me—something I hadn't felt in quite a while.

But two things were out of my control. My dad's

veto power over any of my decisions and EJ's willingness to continue representing me through her father's firm despite her job in California.

Either one could upend my vision.

Chapter Eight
Emma Jane

Dylan's chuckle ran through the line and heated my mushy insides.

"You can't be at the office already."

Seven thirty a.m. was a bit early for me to call anyone, but Dylan had told me he intended to speak to his father last night as soon as he got back to the hotel. And time was of the essence if I wanted to use any sponsorship they'd give as leverage to fast-track the permits.

"No. I'm sitting at my kitchen table having coffee and making a to-do list on the assumption you have good news." My smile hurt my cheeks despite not having received any positive word yet.

"I'll sponsor the fireworks show up to ten thousand dollars. I hope that's sufficient."

"That's wonderful." I jumped up from the table in my exuberance, sloshing coffee all over my yellow legal pad with notes for one of my cases. Then I backtracked. "What do you mean you'll sponsor the fireworks? Won't your company do it?"

"My father was lukewarm on the idea, and I decided not to push. I'd rather save my energy and his goodwill for when it comes time to discuss the soundness of my small-town redevelopment plan."

"Are you sure you want to do this?" Although I

assumed he was financially secure, I knew nothing of his personal finances and didn't want him to invest in Wylder and then regret it. Especially since this donation would not guarantee the issuance of permits.

"I'm sure. But I do want the credit for the sponsorship to go to Addison Redevelopment as well as me. Where do you want the money wired?"

I mopped up the coffee with a paper towel, my initial happiness over this news dulled by the fact that his father wasn't supporting his dream. "I'll ask my mom and get back to you. Thank you so much. Here's hoping it will soften Adam Colton to our permit request."

"EJ, I can hear the concern in your voice. If I didn't want to help out, I wouldn't do it. So please don't worry."

"Okay." I nodded as my heart expanded threefold over his generosity. Not only because he was using his own money, but because he was including his dad's company in the credit.

"What time are you meeting with Adam today?"

"Two." I sighed. "I don't know why people around here always have to have in-person meetings instead of sending an email or picking up the phone. But I guess it's best if I get the news in person. That way, if the decision isn't favorable, I can argue our case without him hanging up on me."

His warm chuckle melted my bones. "Good luck. Let me know as soon as you can."

"Will do. And I'll email you the information this morning on where to send the money for the fireworks."

I hastily showered and dressed, choosing one of my

new frocks from Amber's Boutique—the pink, flowery wrap dress—which I paired with a rose-colored suit jacket and beige pumps to make it look more conservative. Spinning in front of the mirror, I laughed—my new image lifting my spirits. Who knew why I decided to embrace this chicly feminine look? But I wouldn't spend too much time wondering if I was dressing for me or Dylan.

After walking across the backyard to my mother's house, I entered the sunroom where the table was covered with agendas, maps, fliers, and assorted other mystery papers relating to the festival. "Hi, Mom," I called into the kitchen.

"Good morning, honey. Did you stop by for breakfast?"

"No. I don't have time."

I gave my mom a quick kiss, told her the good news, obtained the information I needed for Dylan, and asked her to spread the word immediately about the sponsors for the fireworks.

"Of course I will. I can't believe you were able to do this." Pressing her hand to her chest, she blinked back tears. "I'm so glad you're here. You really are a bright spark in this town, honey." Then she studied me from head to foot. "You look very pretty today. Have you decided to burn your suits?" A grin inched over her mouth.

"Of course not. I need them in San Francisco. But I stopped by Amber's Boutique yesterday and bought a few things. She convinced me to try a new look while I'm here."

"Good for Amber. Did she talk about the wedding?"

"What wedding?"

"Her wedding."

Confusion bounced around in my head. "Amber's engaged? Why didn't I know that? Who is she marrying?" A million more questions threatened to erupt, but I needed answers to the basic ones first before jumping into cross-examination mode.

"She's engaged to Zach Sheridan. It's only been about two weeks now. I'm surprised she didn't tell you. Maybe she thought you'd be upset since your sister dated him in high school."

Little knives stabbed at my heart. Zach had been Ashley's first love, and I was pretty certain Ashley had been Zach's. But time moved on, and serendipitously, Zach and Amber had fallen in love—over thirteen years later. Surely, Amber's silence over this huge life event couldn't be because of my sister's history with Zach. So then why hadn't she shared her good news?

I pushed my bewilderment and hurt feelings aside. Our friendship didn't fall into the category of besties. Our lives had taken completely different paths since high school. But still…

"What is Zach doing these days?" After college, he had worked in Laramie, but clearly, he was back in town.

"He's the editor-in-chief and main journalist for the *Wylder Times*."

"He always did like to write." Memories from high school flew into my consciousness. "Some of his friends would pay him to author their essays for English class. I can't believe Mrs. McCarthy didn't know. I'm sure they all sounded alike. He had a very distinct style."

"You'll probably run into him while you're in town. He seems to be everywhere. You should stop by the newspaper office and tell him about the sponsorship. He's been posting an article a day about the upcoming festival."

"Good idea." Although, in reality, was it? I hadn't seen him in thirteen years, and whenever I pictured him, I saw his haunted eyes and downturned mouth at Ashley's funeral. I'd avoided him during those last few months of senior year, not wanting to share my pain or take on his for fear it would break me. I dug my car keys out of my purse. "I need to get going. I have a lot to do today. See you later."

I worked diligently for a few hours, trying to keep the stress at bay. Waiting on Adam to either grant or deny the permits was nerve-wracking. Hopefully, he wouldn't resort to the past again. Needing to expend some of that angst, I stood and stretched, then decided to go to the coffee shop for a much-needed caffeine boost instead of relying on the office's ancient coffee maker.

"Carol, I'm heading out for a little while. I should be back in a half hour or so."

"Mrs. Applegate called this morning. You met with her and her husband on Tuesday about their wills. She made an appointment for next week to meet with you— that nice secretary who is helping them with their estate planning." Carol's chuckle rang through the reception area.

"So now I'm a secretary? Did they not think the legal advice I gave them rose to the level of an experienced attorney?"

"They're new in town, so they didn't know your

father—or you. And you know how it is sometimes. Especially with some of the older folks. They haven't entered the new age where women are doctors and lawyers and engineers. If given a choice, they'd pick a man to accomplish their needs." She shook her head and tsked.

I bristled as a rash of surliness crept into my chest. "Then make the appointment with Bryce. We'll all be happier."

"Don't take it personally, EJ," she called to my back as I escaped into the bright sunlight of the day.

Everything here was personal to me. I had to develop thicker skin and not allow any hometown burdens, from the past or present, to affect my mission. Mr. and Mrs. Applegate's mistaken impression wasn't what had me so irritable. I knew my worth, and one outlier client wasn't going to dash it. My ill temper grew from the combination of overwhelming emotions brought about by endless mind conversations over Dad, Ashley, Mom, and now Zach and Amber. Not to mention Dylan, a newcomer to the chaos in my head. My psyche was spinning out of control.

I inhaled a long breath to figuratively push away my angst, accompanying my resolution with a powerful rendition of Rachel Platten's "Fight Song"—in my head, of course. My heels clicked along the pavement, providing a beat to accompany my swirling cape of power and strength. I laughed, then let my song drift away as the sun warmed my face and the perfect breeze ruffled my dress.

May in Wylder was a glorious month weather-wise—at least during the day when the temperatures reached into the seventies. Unfortunately, it dipped into the forties at night, but the evening sky was clear enough to see a million stars. Not so in San Francisco. Too many lights, too many buildings. I'd have to take advantage while I was here.

Maybe with Dylan, where we could lie together under the great Wyoming sky, taking in the wonder of nature before our lips met and we spun into our own amazing universe.

I shook my head to dislodge that errant and irrational thought. I should not be fantasizing about stargazing with a near stranger under a canopy of twinkling lights. I'd be gone soon, back to my life in San Francisco, and he'd be doing whatever it was he did every day here in Wylder, or some other small town he deemed ripe for a renovation project. Unless his father pulled him off the project and forced him to return to Chicago.

That would just be too sad, and I couldn't let that happen on my watch.

Had I ever felt this strongly about a client before? Never would be the correct answer. He was working his way too often into my thoughts—and not because he was no-nonsense, unapproachable, and demanding. I had seen a more vulnerable side to him when he shared his dream of helping small towns regenerate. He wanted to make a difference in people's lives, not merely work to add more cement to big cities.

But the gesture that really endeared him to me was using his own money to sponsor the fireworks. He was taking a huge leap of faith not only in our community, but in my advice. He knew the issuance of permits was not connected to his donation. Yet he had chosen to invest in my town. Well…my old town.

He deserved as much time and attention to his project as I could afford. We had to make his hotel a success.

After breezing into Hannah's Blend Coffee Shop, I ordered a medium roast before notifying Hannah, in a loud enough voice so those sitting at the counter and nearby tables would also be informed, that Wylder would have a fireworks show next Saturday, thanks to Dylan Addison. The happy murmurs assured me the word would spread.

My next stop was the *Wylder Times* office. I approached the young woman at the front desk and asked for Zach Sheridan. Without requesting my name, she yelled, "Hey, Zach, someone's here to see you."

No one appeared. I waited for a few minutes, but patience was not my forte. I had a hundred things to do and limited time in which to do them. "Excuse me. Do you know whether Zach heard you?"

The woman huffed a sigh and got up, disappearing down the hall. Within seconds, Zach came to the front, looking a little rumpled but very much like the handsome boy my sister had a thing for in high school. He sported faded jeans, a flannel shirt, and unpolished boots—the uniform of the men in this town.

"EJ! What brings you here?" His smile welcomed me, and none of the desolation from so long ago appeared on his face.

"Hi, Zach. My mom said you were the editor-in-chief. Very impressive."

He chuckled. "Yep. I'm in charge of myself and two part-time reporters."

Small-town newspapers were important, but with the internet, circulation had to be falling off, just like in the larger cities. Hopefully, Wylder was a decade or two behind everyone else.

"I was in Amber's shop yesterday. We spent at least an hour together, but it wasn't until my mom told me this morning that I learned the two of you are engaged. Congratulations. I couldn't be happier for you. Or her."

He beamed. "Thanks. She's incredible. I can't believe it took me so long to see her as more than a friend. I lucked out when she agreed to marry me."

I slanted my head, taking in the tall, sandy-haired man who had starred in my sister's fantasies. "She has too."

A blush crept up his neck. "Thanks."

"I stopped by not only to congratulate you, but to let you know that we have a sponsor for the fireworks next Saturday. Dylan Addison and his company, Addison Redevelopment Corp., are footing the bill." I inwardly cringed at my bald promotion of a client. In San Francisco, my clients had their own public-relations machines spitting out relevant and helpful press. This was not their lawyer's job.

"That's great. I'll give him a shout-out in tomorrow's edition." He frowned. "Are you on the festival committee? I heard you were back, but I assumed it was for a week or two, as usual."

"Your assumption would be correct. I'm helping out at the firm for a couple of weeks. And no, I'm not on the committee. But my mom's the co-chair, as you probably are aware." I decided further explanation was required. "I represent, or more specifically, my dad's firm represents Dylan and the Wylder Hotel. I'm introducing him around and getting him involved so he's not treated as an out-of-towner."

He nodded. "It'll take more than sponsoring fireworks, but it's a great start. If you want, why don't you bring him by the Five Star tonight at eight? I'm meeting Amber, and there's a fantastic country band playing. We can toast to old times and new. And it will be good to meet him."

Better than good. Zach knew everyone in town and held the reins to the news that got printed. Dylan making friends with Zach could only help him in the long run.

"Perfect. And it will give me a chance to catch up more with Amber." And find out why she hadn't told me she was engaged. "See you tonight."

Hopefully, by then we'd also have the permits to celebrate.

Chapter Nine
Emma Jane

At one forty-five I walked to the municipal building to meet with Adam Colton, my feet heavy as I bolstered my plan to sway him if his initial ruling wasn't favorable. Dylan had so much riding on these permits that I had to do everything I could to make it happen. And even though I'd only stepped in to help temporarily, I felt the burden of this legal problem weighing on my shoulders.

In representing my clients in San Francisco, I'd been in similar positions, dealing with not only government red tape, but community uproars forcing me to take my clients' causes to court when the initial outcome wasn't favorable. Dylan didn't have time for that. And neither did I. Almost one week into my so-called vacation, I had limited days to shine as his white knight.

In no time I stood at the counter in the permit office waiting for Colton to appear.

"Right on time, EJ. How's it going?" His smile seemed a little sinister, but that might just have been my pessimistic interpretation.

"Good, Adam. How about with you?" If small talk worked, so be it. "Did you hear that Dylan Addison is sponsoring the fireworks for the Spring Festival?" I might as well jump right in with the good news. "He's saving the event."

"I heard. Smart advising, Counselor. Your father would have suggested the same if he were in the predicament you're in. But then again, if your father was still involved—"

He didn't finish the sentence, but I presumed he was telling me, without admitting to anything inappropriate, that the permits would have been issued already.

Ire wound through me like a snake, but I needed to keep my cool. He hadn't come right out and said that the issuance of permits depended on who represented the client. He was probably trying to push my buttons to get back at me for losing the debate championship.

"If what you're insinuating is true"—I kept a smile pasted to my lips—"then I'm assuming you're about to hand me the permits."

"No. Your assumption would be wrong. In following the strict regulations dealing with the addition Mr. Addison wants to make, he will need to go to the planning board. But in the spirit of goodwill and a nod to our acquaintance, albeit strained, I will put this matter on the planning board's agenda for their next meeting—June second—even though you missed the deadline. The board meets at six p.m. I'll give you until Monday to submit your paperwork." He bowed as if he were handing me a gift.

My stomach fell, and I bit my tongue to prevent any venomous words from escaping. I knew Dylan needed approval from the planning board if we followed the letter of the law. I'd already tried to dance around that rule when I was here a few days ago. But the optimistic side of my brain had made me believe

Adam would change course.

"I appreciate your generosity in placing us on the schedule, but I have to be back in San Francisco by May twenty-fifth. Is it possible to call an emergency meeting for next week?"

I was grasping for a lifeline; I knew my boss would deny me more time. The Briar real estate closing was coming up, and although I worked on it every night, some things could only be done while present in the city.

"Sorry, EJ. Can't do that. The only other option is to put you on the agenda for their next meeting, which is over three months from now. If that works out better for you because of your schedule, that's what I'll do."

"No, no, that's not necessary." Panic infiltrated my words. Three months would be a bullet to Dylan's gut. "We'll take the slot for the next meeting." I paused, considering whether to ask the question on the tip of my tongue. "What are the chances the board will approve the permits at the meeting?"

He shrugged. "Don't know. That's up to them."

"Of course." I inhaled. "I thought that perhaps you had your finger on their pulse. Thank you for putting us on the next agenda." *Be nice, be nice, be nice.* Hopefully, another two and half weeks wouldn't kill Dylan's project.

"There's one condition you'll need to meet in order to reserve that spot."

His gleeful smile unnerved me. What vengeful hoop would I have to jump through to smooth over our troubled rapport? "You mean in addition to having the paperwork in by Monday?" How much worse could this get?

"Yes. But it's not something you'll hate. As a matter of fact, you should enjoy it."

If he suggested we have dinner together, I was going to vomit right on the counter separating us. "What is it?" I held my breath, my teeth cutting into my lower lip.

"We need two more workers to man the ring toss at the festival. You and Dylan will be perfect. I'm surprised I didn't see your name on the list of volunteers already. Especially since your mom is running the show."

I exhaled. At least his request wasn't as traumatic as I'd anticipated. And, shockingly, it was something I would enjoy. "You got it."

"Great. See you Monday when you drop off the papers for the planning board."

"Since we're getting along so well, can I have until Wednesday?"

He chuckled good-naturedly. "Fine. See you Wednesday."

He turned and strode back to his office as I readjusted the moving pieces of my far-too-busy schedule.

Chapter Ten
Dylan

I paced outside of the municipal building as the minutes ticked by. Having arrived at five after two so as not to run into EJ when she got there, I hadn't counted on her meeting with Adam Colton to take more than a few minutes. Although I knew she'd call as soon as she could, I figured this would make it easier. She could hand me the permits or lay out the verdict as I walked her back to the office.

She emerged at two twenty. Was that a good sign or bad? No smile of victory bloomed on her face. But she didn't look disconcerted either—although her head was down and her lips moved in a silent conversation with herself.

Dressed in a pink, floral frock, she looked like a flower herself—delicate, willowy, beautiful. Despite her outward appearance, I knew her inner strength channeled power and determination—the contrast very appealing.

"EJ. Hi."

She startled, then focused on me. "Dylan, what are you doing here?"

"I'm anxious about the outcome and didn't want to wait for your call." *And I wanted to see you again.*

She walked closer, then stopped a few feet away. "Well, there's good news and bad news." She was quick to add, "The bad news isn't so bad."

"Go on." I steeled myself.

"I don't have your permits. Yet. You're scheduled to go before the planning board on June second. Generally, we would have to wait for the following meeting, which is over three months from now, but Adam said he'd add your matter to the schedule. He's doing us a huge favor."

"Okay." I kept my disappointment over the news hidden. "That's good, I guess. Right? Do you foresee any problem with the board?"

"I can't imagine that they don't want the Wylder Hotel to be up and running as soon as possible. When Bryce explains that you're only adding storage space onto the kitchen area, it should be a simple yes vote."

"What do you mean when Bryce explains it?" Anxiety twisted my gut. "You're my lawyer."

She lowered her lids, then looked past my shoulder. "I'm only here for another week or so. I can't stay until June."

I caught her gaze, and a host of emotions stormed through those beautiful eyes.

"I'm sorry, Dylan. I have a job back in San Francisco. My boss fought against me taking these two weeks. If I ask her for more time, she just might fire me."

I thought she'd be here longer. I thought she'd at least consider taking over her dad's firm. She'd agreed to represent me. None of this was making sense. "When do you have to be back?"

"May twenty-fifth. The meeting is eight days later."

"Then you simply need to add another week. You

said you've been working on your cases from here. Another eight days can't make that much difference. EJ, will you please stay and meet with the planning board? I need you there. Not Bryce."

Her confession that she was returning to San Francisco in a week's time had my mind short-circuiting.

I reached out to touch her arm, as if the physical connection would sway her. Or maybe it's what I needed to quiet the riot of problems swirling in my brain. My father had given me to the end of the month to get the permits before he pulled the plug on the project. The board meeting was two days later, not an insurmountable problem, but there was still no guarantee I'd get the permits after the hearing. EJ was carefully placing me back in Bryce's hands despite my objections. And I had no clue what her plan was with regard to the firm going forward.

"I'm confused. I thought you were here to help. I didn't realize your assistance had an expiration date." I held my tongue further, afraid my frustration would come out as anger.

"I did come to help. And to figure out how best to deal with this overwhelming situation." She opened her mouth as if to say more, then closed it.

Then it hit me. "Are you selling the practice?"

"Shhh." She looked around to assure no one else heard me. "It's a possibility. But I don't want anyone to know. I can't have our clients leaving the firm before any potential sale. The business would be worthless."

The anger did kick in then, and heat streamed up my neck. "So you're stringing me along, hoping to keep me satisfied as a client until a sale goes through?"

She didn't duck her head or glance past me in embarrassment. She looked me straight in the eyes. "I'm not stringing you along. I'm doing everything in my power to represent you to the best of my ability. I'm on your side, Dylan. I don't even know if there is a potential buyer for the firm out there. I'm reviewing all possibilities, trying to do what's best for my mother. As well as what's best for our clients."

Her fire and spirit burned through my exasperation, and I was the one who bent my head awkwardly. I selfishly wanted her to stay, not only to represent me, but to see if those sparks she set off in my blood would ignite into a blazing inferno. "You're right. I'm sorry. You have to do what's best for your mom."

"And for the clients," she added.

Her features softened, and I could almost feel her aura wrap around me in a comforting cloak.

I accepted her response for the time being, slipping my hands firmly into my pockets to keep from stealing another touch, but it didn't stop me from looking into those magnificent irises. What I really wanted to do at that moment was capture her lips with mine and sweep her up into my world so she wouldn't want to leave. Ever. But that seemed an unlikely outcome.

I held her gaze, quiet moments filling the air as I sent hopeful pleas to her soul.

Charged seconds elapsed before she eased back a step, biting her lip and disconnecting from our private force field. "I'll call my boss and request more time, but I already know the answer."

I exhaled and nodded, accepting her effort as the best I could get right now.

"There's a condition we have to meet in order to

get on the next board meeting agenda." Her slow grin advised me it couldn't be too bad.

"What is it?"

"We have to work one of the games at the festival next Saturday."

This unpredicted stipulation caused a bubble of laughter to burst out—not an unwelcome feeling given the host of emotions I'd just experienced. Spending the day with EJ at the festival would most assuredly ease the pain of not getting anything that I wanted right now—the permits, her future representation, her decision to stay.

"It would be my pleasure."

We walked back to her office, with EJ filling me in on the breadth of the festival and what it meant to the community.

"I almost forgot." She stopped short. "Zach Sheridan, the editor of the *Wylder Times*, invited us to meet him and his fiancée, Amber—who just happens to be a friend of mine from high school—at the Five Star Saloon tonight at eight. Can you make it?"

The huge disappointment over her confession collided with joy in my gut. "I can." We still had a week left to work together, maybe more if her boss was feeling generous. And we also had that time to play together.

"Good. Put your dancing boots on because there's a band." She smiled over her shoulder as she entered her office. "See you there, cowboy."

I stood out on the sidewalk with an uncontrollable grin taking over my face.

Chapter Eleven
Emma Jane

I slid into my office chair and exhaled, berating myself for letting the potential sale of the practice come out that way. Especially with Dylan. He was under a tremendous amount of pressure, courtesy of his father, and I didn't want to be the one to pull the rug out from under him while he teetered to stay standing.

The look on his face—disappointment, anxiety, regret?—had made me want to caress his tightened jaw and kiss his full lips until he forgot all about permits, planning boards, renovations, and contracts. Every time he touched me, I wanted to take those fingers that could fan desire with the tiniest stroke against my palm and slide them all over my heated skin.

Dylan Addison was creeping into my heart and soul, but I so wanted him to take over my body as well. Daydreams. Fantasies. Desires.

All for naught.

I was leaving, and he was staying. Or not. Depending on the fate of the Wylder Hotel.

Pushing him from my thoughts with much effort, I worked until seven thirty. Then I dashed into the ladies' room, pulled my hair up into a high ponytail, dabbed on some lip gloss and blush, and twirled before the mirror to appreciate my fluttering dress. If Amber were here, she'd advise me to lose the conservative jacket and add some jewelry, small changes that would shift my outfit from day to evening. I ignored her mental advice while studying my appearance a little more skeptically, shaking my head at the pink flowery attire. *Who are you?* Yet a smile hijacked my mouth.

I walked the few blocks over to the Five Star and could hear the crowd from half a block away. When I stepped inside, the heat enveloped me, and the noise level increased with laughter, shouting, and the beginning strings of the band warming up.

Looking past the packed bar, I caught Chad's eye and yelled, "Have you seen Amber and Zach?"

He pointed to a booth closer to the dance floor.

I mouthed my thanks and squeezed through the throngs to my destination. "Hi, you two. You must have gotten here at six to get a seat."

Amber patted the bench next to her. "We came for dinner, knowing it would get crowded."

"I should go stand near the door and wait for Dylan. If I don't grab him, he might turn around and leave once he sees how packed this place is."

I didn't get the impression his Friday nights included a mob scene at a local pub. He seemed more likely to be part of the designer-suit-wearing, limo-riding, private-club-attending set where the liquor was top shelf, the ambiance a reserved din, and the dress decidedly upscale. At least that's the way I pictured him in Chicago, thanks to *Business USA*.

The heat of too many bodies mashing into a crowded space convinced me to take off my jacket before making my way to the front.

"Nice dress." Amber beamed. "It looks great. Dylan will love it." A knowing look accompanied her smirk.

I responded with a sassy wink. "I'll be back. Can I get you something from the bar while I'm up?"

"We ordered a pitcher and four glasses, so we're all set unless you want something different."

"Perfect." I didn't want to wrestle with the crowd anyway, and who knew how long it would be before Chad would have a moment to take my order?

Interesting how at times I felt as if I'd never left Wylder, falling easily into conversations with the people of the town as if I hadn't been gone since I graduated from high school. Yet, at other times, I'd felt as much of an outsider as Dylan must have felt.

The door opened, and several more people entered with Dylan at the rear. My heart fluttered as I watched his eyes dart around the bar, taking in the chaos as he stuck close to the entrance. His six two frame was outfitted in Levi's, belted in leather, and a blue-and-gray flannel shirt. Replacing his highly polished boots were a pair made from genuine rawhide. I smiled. He'd finally read the memo. But whether dressed in designer clothes or cowboy duds, he was one spectacular-looking man.

"Dylan," I called through the crowd and waved while inching closer to him.

His smile dazzled and sent my heart tripping over itself. Did he have that effect on all women?

We met in the middle, and I took his hand, still worried that he could make a mad dash out of the place at any moment. Those now-familiar zings travelled up my arm and through my system as his hand settled in mine. A perfect fit.

Chad's voice cut through the din. "Hey, Dylan my

man. I hear you're sponsoring the fireworks for the Spring Festival."

He nodded, a flash of red creeping into his cheeks.

"That's great. Everybody, turn around. This is Dylan Addison, the new owner of the Wylder Hotel and savior of our celebration next Saturday night."

The crowd clapped, cheered, whistled, and those nearby slapped him on the back along with their thanks. This couldn't have been staged any better.

I inched closer to his ear so I wasn't shouting my words. "I told you Chad was a good messenger."

He squeezed my hand in reply and whispered his acknowledgement, sending dancing butterflies over my lobe and down my neck where his breath floated over sensitized skin. He was so close I could inhale his scent—cedar and musk—an aphrodisiac in itself. No touching necessary.

I turned my head to take in those beautiful crystal blues, but my gaze got lost on his lips, dangerously close to mine.

Lowering my lids to fight off temptation, I backed away, hoping to dowse the fire igniting in my core. I then pulled him toward the booth where Amber and Zach sat. "These are my friends from high school."

After the perfunctory greetings and handshakes, we sat, removed from the restless crowds bumping into each other, and with a somewhat private space for conversation. Zach and Dylan hit it off immediately, with Dylan questioning Zach about the health of the other businesses in town, the need for a nice hotel and restaurant, and the merits of small-town life. I didn't doubt that Zach would eventually interview Dylan for a nice article in the paper, sharing the plans for his hotel and creating an excellent buzz.

While the men talked, I turned to Amber. "Did you forget to tell me yesterday that you were engaged to Zach?" I gave her my sternest look, but a smile broke through. "My mom told me this morning. I'm so happy for you."

A sweet blush covered her cheeks. "I know I should have. I wanted to. But you had a lot on your mind, and I didn't know how you would take it. Sharing that piece of news while you tried on dresses didn't seem like the appropriate time."

"Were you holding back because Zach dated Ashley in high school?" My voice had turned soft, almost reverent when I said my twin's name.

She nodded. "Part of the reason."

"That was a long time ago. They were kids." Unfortunately, Ashley would never be older than that.

"I know, I know. I planned to tell you when we got together for drinks next week. But your mother beat me to it." Sadness and remorse flitted through her gray eyes.

"I appreciate your considering my feelings. But Ashley died a long time ago, and of course Zach was going to move on. I'm so glad he's doing it with you. What was the other part of the reason you failed to tell me your exciting news?"

She sighed. "It all happened so fast. One day we were friends, and the next day we'd become…more. It was right after your dad died. Zach was so sad. He and your dad were on several town committees together and genuinely liked each other. Of course, everyone loved your dad." She looked into my eyes, sharing her sorrow with me. "I wanted to comfort him. As a friend. But one thing led to another. Next thing you know, we were inseparable. We'd only been seeing each other for six weeks before he proposed." Amber's entire being glowed.

"If you had shared this amazing love story with me the other day, it would have buoyed my spirits, and I wouldn't have been sulking over all the work I had to do."

"I was afraid you'd think I was crazy to agree to marry him so quickly after just getting together."

My smile bloomed from within. "I am thrilled for you and Zach. It's not easy to find the right person. But when you know, you know. And you two clearly know. So when's the big day?"

"We want to have our reception at the Wylder Hotel, so we're waiting to hear when it will open. Probably in the fall."

"That's wonderful. It will be so special."

"Now that you know and you're not telling me how crazy I am to get engaged so fast, I'm hoping you'll be able to attend."

"I'd be honored."

"Even though you live in San Francisco and we're not as close as we used to be, I still count you as the one person I could go to if I really needed something." She took my hand and squeezed it.

Zach cut into our lovefest. "It looks like you two are long-lost relatives. I hate to break this up, but it's time to dance."

The band had segued into "She's Country," beckoning the crowd to join in.

"Let's do it." Amber beamed at him, love glowing on her face.

I slid from the booth to let her out, and Dylan did the same for Zach.

"While we're both standing, would you like to dance?" he asked.

I glanced over to the dance floor, and couples were doing the two-step. "I'd love to. I didn't pin you as a country dancer." Or any kind of dancer for that matter. His serious demeanor made me think frivolity was far down his to-do list.

"I like that I can surprise you." He took my elbow and steered me to an open spot.

We slid easily into the dance, and a grin seized my mouth. In high school, my girlfriends and I had loved to dance, and we'd take over the floor at school events. Eventually, the boys would join us because that's how they got to hold a girl.

Dylan's arm wound around my waist as we moved forward, then he spun me out and back toward him with the ease of a professional. The heat of his hand inched up my back and inward, firing up my blood with this intimacy. Something about him reached into my soul and hugged it.

He wasn't at all what I'd expected. When I first met him, I'd assumed he was an obnoxiously demanding client who used his father's name to push forth his agenda. But now I knew his assertiveness came from his ambition to make a difference. And to show his father what one project could do for a town like ours. But most surprisingly, he was loyal. He hadn't fled the firm when Dad died, instead giving us time to come up for air. When he learned there was a possibility that we'd sell the firm, he hadn't jumped ship. At least not yet. And even though he knew his sponsorship of the fireworks wouldn't guarantee his permits would be issued quickly, he'd done it anyway, using his own funds.

His kind soul raised his attractiveness bar to eleven, and I was powerless to stop the swirling emotions his presence evoked.

When the song was over, the band transitioned to a slow dance. He pulled me into his arms and smiled. "This is a nice way of getting to know each other better."

His honeyed baritone oozed straight to my heart.

I knew, deep down, I couldn't let myself fall. I'd be leaving soon, and long-distance relationships never worked. Especially with two driven people trying to make a name for themselves in their respective circles. Not that he'd so much as suggested such a thing.

I avoided his eyes and instead looked over his shoulder, but the warmth of his body against mine was making it difficult.

Conversation might help. "I saw that the mayor is here. I want to introduce you. Let's go." I started to pull away from his embrace, but he held me tighter.

"There's time."

His gaze caught mine, and I fell into the abyss of aqua pools. Strong fingers splayed over the small of my back, keeping me blissfully in his orbit as we swayed to the music of a love song. I inhaled his cedar scent, never wanting to forget this feeling of floating, no matter how inconvenient. Or untimely.

The song ended, and he brought my hand up to his mouth and grazed my fingers with his lips. "Thank you for the dance."

Bodies moved around us, but I was totally

immersed in the Dylan zone. Until someone bumped me, pushing me out of my trance.

"Sorry, EJ. Welcome home, by the way."

I looked at the speaker. "Hi, Tim. Oh. Dylan, this is our mayor, Tim Drucker. Tim, this is Dylan Addison. Have the two of you met?"

Tim responded. "No. I haven't had the pleasure, but I've been hearing your name around town. Of course, I knew you bought the Wylder Hotel. But I also heard you're sponsoring the fireworks for the Spring Festival." He pumped Dylan's hand in an enthusiastic shake. "Thank you so much. We really appreciate it, given the belt-tightening we had to do this year. Let's set up a meeting sometime next week so you can tell me about your plans for the hotel."

"Great. I would love to discuss it." Dylan reached into his back pocket and pulled out a business card. Ever the professional. "Let me know when you have the time." He handed Tim the card.

"Will do." Then Tim turned to me. "I'm glad to see you're taking care of the legal needs of our townspeople."

"Oh. I'm only here for a short time. To help Bryce out." My standard line, which Dylan now knew was not totally true. "But of course, I'll continue to do whatever I can to fill the huge hole my father left."

"Your father was a great man. We really miss him." His tone was somber and his eyes saddened. "I know I said it before, but I'm truly sorry for your loss. I'm sure you looked forward to practicing with him."

Another punch to the gut. "Yes." My throat tightened, and I could say no more.

Dylan must have keyed in to my grief. "Good to

meet you, Mayor. We'll talk more next week."

He took my arm and led me back to the table as I tried to clear my blurry vision.

"Thanks for ending that conversation." I slid into my side of the booth, and Dylan sat across from me.

"Would you like to leave? We can go to the bar at the Vincent House, which should be quieter."

"I had wanted to be out with the crowds tonight so I could introduce you around. But I think I would like to leave if you're okay with that." Melancholy had taken a strong hold over my initial lightheartedness.

He stood. "I'll go tell Zach and Amber we're leaving. Not that they'd notice." He chuckled as he headed to the dance floor to say good-bye for both of us.

Out on the street, a cool night breeze ruffled my dress, and I slid my arms into my jacket. "I don't want to sound forward, but we can go back to my place for a drink. It will assure that we don't run into anyone else that will pick at the scab of my father's death."

"Good with me. Let's get my car, and I'll drive you to yours, then follow you there."

This day had had so many zigzags I wasn't sure where my scrambled emotions would settle. But having Dylan to myself to end the day, even though I intellectually knew it was a bad idea, was the one bright star that could lift me out of my funk.

Chapter Twelve
Emma Jane

"Come on into my tiny abode." I led Dylan into the guest cottage behind my mom's house—my second home. It was perfect for my needs and my privacy—a four-room dwelling that contained a living room, bedroom, bathroom, and kitchenette.

"Let me take your coat." I held out my hand to receive the butter-soft leather jacket he'd put on once we got to his car—the cool night temperature requiring it. The brush of his fingers against mine sent electricity from limb to limb, reminding me of his magnetic force. As if I needed reminding.

I opened the front closet, empty except for a few lone hangers and a huge wooden board polished to a mahogany sheen. After hanging his jacket, I used both hands to grip the plank and pull it out. I turned it and gasped.

"What is it?" He looked over my shoulder.

"It's a sign to hang outside the law office." Tears stung my eyes. *Hampton and Hampton, Attorneys at Law.* "My father must have had this made for the day I'd join him in his practice." Sorrow beat a path to my heart.

Dylan's warm hands massaged my shoulders. "Don't beat yourself up over this. You weren't ready. I'm sure your father knew that."

I sighed as I put the sign back in the closet. "He was so patient. So understanding. Never pressuring me to come home."

"He was a classy guy, and he sounds like a wonderful, supportive father. He wouldn't have wanted you to have any regrets." He raised my chin with his fingers and underscored his message with serious eyes.

"You're right. But I never told him the real reason it was so hard for me to return."

A frown furrowed his brow. "Would you like to share it with me?"

His quiet question reached into my soul. At this moment, I would tell him anything.

"I had a sister. A twin. She died in a car accident at the hands of a drunk driver when we were seniors in high school." I could hear the rasp in my voice, the pain that still surfaced when I recalled that traumatic event. "We had big plans. We were both going to go to law school after college, work for a year or two to get experience, then come back to Wylder to practice law. Together with my dad. A family business. We talked about it for years, starting when we were little and playing at being lawyers, throughout high school when we were both on the debate team. It was our dream."

I saw the sympathy deep in his eyes—etched on his face. But with him, I didn't rebuild my walls and shut down. He made me want to share this burden, this sorrow. "Because I could no longer return to practice law with Ashley, I felt it would be disloyal to carry on with our plan without her. I thought that, eventually, I'd be able to see my way back here. Unfortunately, time ran out."

He enfolded me in his arms and hugged me.

"You've been carrying around this secret for a long time, protecting your pact with Ashley. But she will always be with you, no matter where you live or where you work. She's your twin. She would have understood any decision you made."

His voice reverberated against my chest, filling me with his wisdom.

"Maybe it's time to think about what it is you want, without worrying about your father's wishes or your unfulfilled dream with Ashley."

As his words wound around me, the oddest feeling swept through my heart. Release came with his comforting thoughts. Solid and masculine, he wove a protective blanket around me that held me together—straighter and stronger and tougher.

I breathed in his scent, his strength, before moving away, trying out my new armor. A smile inched over my lips. "Thank you for listening…without judgment. And for reminding me that Ashley is always with me."

"Of course." His voice, his eyes, his heart were intoxicating.

I needed some space from the man who was slipping into my soul, so I inhaled and reverted to playing hostess. "What would you like to drink? I have red wine—a cabernet—or vodka. Not sure why that's in the cabinet when there's nothing else."

"Wine is good if you're having some."

I went into the kitchenette, separated from the living room by a counter with stools, and placed the wine, glasses, and corkscrew on the granite surface. I spread my hand over the cool material, hoping its physicality would ground my swirling emotions.

My gaze strayed to his wide shoulders and tapered

back, usually covered in fine cotton custom shirts, but now sporting blue plaid flannel. A nod to my advice. He studied a framed photograph on the wall.

"Who's this?" He pointed to an older woman dressed in black, her gray hair in a neat bun at the base of her head.

"I can't believe that photo made its way to this cottage." I uncorked the wine and poured. "Back in the late eighteen hundreds, my great-great-great-grandmother on my mother's side—I'm not sure I have enough greats in there—was a judge in South Pass City, Wyoming—one of the first female judges in the state."

"Impressive." He came over to sit on a stool.

"Can you imagine being a woman judge back then? I know I can't. Some of the people in this town still don't think women can be lawyers." I clinked my glass against his. "To Esther McQuigg."

"I agree that small towns can be several decades behind when it comes to women's rights. Other people's rights too. So how did Esther become a judge?"

"They were called justices of the peace back then. The county board of commissioners appointed her after the previous justice resigned in protest over the passage of the women's suffrage amendment."

I stood in the kitchenette, the counter separating us. This little history lesson would take my mind off more seductive thoughts like staring into his crystal-blue eyes or running my fingers over the planes of his handsome face. "Of course, she had no legal training, and she held court in her living room. I heard she was tough in her attempt to keep order in a town that had drifters, outlaws, gamblers, and carpetbaggers in addition to the local ranchers, farmers, and miners. She only held that position for a year because the term was up. The story goes that her husband was against her appointment from the beginning. He made such a huge scene in her courtroom one day that she had him jailed." I laughed at the picture I painted. "What power."

"Have you ever thought of following in her footsteps?"

"You mean being a judge?"

"Maybe. More like coming back to the area where your ancestors have lived for over a hundred years. It would be an amazing circle to complete if you did repeat that bit of history by taking on that role."

I chuckled. "Interesting." *But not going to happen.*

After moving around the counter, I sat on the stool next to Dylan. Perhaps not a wise decision given the unrelenting and hypnotic hold he had over me. My knee brushed against his, and that minutest of touches sent fire racing through my blood.

He took the wine from my hand and set both glasses on the counter. "Thank you for tonight." He placed his warm hands on my face, intense cerulean eyes keying into my soul. His lips were kissing close. All I had to do was lean in.

So I did.

The press of my lips against his started out chaste and tentative but within seconds turned hot and passionate. His tongue mated with mine, sending me swirling into an eddy of pleasure. His palms seared my waist as he pulled me from sitting to standing, our bodies aligning in a tactile embrace. I moved my hands up his solid chest, feeling the soft flannel of his shirt, the tensing of his muscles beneath. He deepened the kiss, taking my breath away. My fingers drifted up his shoulders, and I wrapped my arms around his neck, seeking the strength of his body to touch every part of me from mouth to torso to legs to toes. His sultry scent sparked my libido, arousing every cell and atom in my being.

My subconscious niggled at me to stop the freefall, but I couldn't. Didn't want to. This feeling sent me to the heavens, and no one in their right mind would want to leave.

His mouth drifted to my ear, then my neck, awakening all my erogenous zones with a carnal invitation. I sighed as his fingers fluttered down my neck, his knuckles brushing against my clavicle, the swell of my breasts.

I could feel his heart beating, his breathing quickening. Pushing my hands up under his shirt, I relished his heat, his toned abs, his moan when I moved my hand lower to ease the strap of his belt through the buckle.

He grasped my hand to stop me, his voice raspy. "Are you sure you want to do this?"

"Oh, I'm sure." At that moment, I had never been more sure about anything in my life.

I'd worry about the consequences of diving into a sexual relationship with a near stranger some other time. No one in my past had ever ignited me the way he did, from our first meeting three days ago—despite my unflattering assumptions about him—until this very moment. Blinded by lust, all I wanted to do was feel him, smell him, taste him.

And make love to him.

Taking his hand in mine, I drew him to my

bedroom, but the space between us on the short walk was unbearable. I slipped into his embrace and connected with sensuous eyes, sparking with hunger and need.

This was insane. I knew it. He probably knew it too. But I was willing to fall head first into insanity if it meant taking this incredible plunge into paradise.

His hot palms caressed my face before he dragged flitting fingers down my neck and to the sensitized underside of my arms. He slowly untied the fabric at my hip that held my dress together, and as the material fell open, the pink lace of my bra appeared. Trailing fingers traced the lace over the swell of my breast before he rubbed his thumb over my nipple. I bit my lip, dying to fling my dress to the floor yet savoring the sensual torture he bestowed.

With nimble fingers, I unbuttoned his shirt and slid my hands over corrugated muscles and hot skin, pressing my nose against his chest to breathe in his pure-Dylan scent. His abs tightened as my hands wandered lower, brushing my palm over the button of his jeans, then the thick bulge below.

His breath hitched, and his lids lowered before he grabbed my wrist and moved it away. "You're killing me," he rasped.

"That was my intent." I smiled as I grazed my lips over the seam of his, pressing my breasts against his bare chest.

He grasped my hips and pulled me against the swollen ridge of his erection, grinding against the sensitized area between my legs, our clothing still a barrier between us.

With a heightened sense of urgency, he slid my

dress down my arms, letting it fall to the floor before splaying his hands over my satin-covered rear. Tingles danced over every surface of my skin as his tongue plunged into my mouth with fiery passion. Cool air and hot hands washed over my body with only my bra and panties preventing total sensory immersion.

His slick tongue stroked my neck, sending goose bumps to every pore, as his hands cupped and fondled my breasts, pulling at my nipples through the fabric of my bra. My back arched, giving him full access, begging him to continue his onslaught as I threaded my fingers through silky hair.

He released the clasp of my bra and banished it to the floor, his hot, wet mouth replacing the fire of his hands. Long fingers deftly played with the elastic of my panties before slipping inside and stroking my sensitive flesh. A moan escaped as desire leapt and pulsated through every nerve. My frenzied hands gripped solid shoulders, but I needed to feel more—all of him. I inched away and immediately yearned for his devouring mouth on my pebbled peaks, but I'd invite him back once his clothes were missing.

Fingers trembling with adrenaline, I tugged his belt from its confining loops before dropping it on the floor next to my dress. Then I got to work on his zipper, pushing the course denim down his legs, then doing the same with his briefs. I turned to yank the comforter and top sheet off the bed, craving the cool linen to compete with the heat rolling off my body.

Dylan stood next to the bed, his gaze sweeping across my reclining form. "You're beautiful," he murmured, his voice husky.

I raked my gaze over his hard, tight body, his

impressive erection. "So are you." I reached my hand to his and drew him to me.

He gently dragged my panties down my legs and tossed them on the heap, then sheathed himself in a condom before joining me. "I've been fantasizing about you all week. This is so much better." He hovered over me, holding himself up with sinewed arms as he kissed my forehead, my cheeks, my eyes, my nose before whispering over my mouth with exquisite lips.

I snaked my arms around his neck, then pulled him on top of me, feeling my breasts crush into his chest, the rigid length of his manhood against my stomach. I opened my legs, and he teased my sensitive folds, a tumult of swirling senses surging through me. "I want you...I need you inside of me."

His low groan told me he wanted to be there too. He guided his shaft to my opening and nudged inside ever so slowly until his entire length filled me up. Moving deliberately at first, allowing me to savor every arousing stroke, he increased his rhythm until I couldn't see, couldn't think, couldn't process anything but the building current of my orgasm. His pounding thrusts exploded within, and my muscles contracted around him as wave after wave of cascading pleasure shattered me. Even before my tremors ceased, he gripped me tightly and plunged in hard and fast as he found his ecstasy.

I floated in an orgasmic haze. But was the best sex I'd ever had in my life the result of lust or love?

Chapter Thirteen
Emma Jane

The next morning, I crept out of bed at six and softly closed the bedroom door behind me so as not to awaken Dylan. I needed to work on my major closing since the last few days had me otherwise occupied. I sat at the small table between the living room and kitchen and focused on what needed to be done.

Just as the sun was starting to shine through the window next to me, I felt warm hands kneading my shoulders. That one touch awakened my libido and threatened to steal my mind and body.

"What time did you wake up?"

His husky voice buzzed through me. I smiled and leaned back into his massage, moaning with pleasure. "Six. What time is it now?"

"A little after eight. You could have wakened me."

"We didn't get to sleep until after two. And you were totally dead to the world at six. Besides, I needed to get some work done, and if I woke you, we both know that wouldn't have happened."

His warm chuckle surrounded me in contented bliss.

"Very true." He kissed the top of my head and moved into the kitchen to pour coffee from the pot I'd started earlier. "Do you have any eggs here? I'll make them."

"Sorry. No. I never made it to the grocery store. I usually go to my mom's house to eat if I want something. Which I don't think we should do this morning." I didn't want to shock her with his presence before explaining what was happening. Although I hadn't a clue what my explanation would be.

"I'll run into town to get something. What would you like?"

My insides bubbled with happiness that he wasn't preparing to go back to his suite at the hotel and leave me—now that our night of ecstasy was over. Today was Saturday, and I wanted nothing more than to spend the day with him—once I finished my work.

"I'll take an egg-and-cheese sandwich with bacon, please." My smile split my face.

"You got it. I'll be back soon." He buttoned his shirt, much to my disappointment.

"What are you doing today?" A twinge of anxiety worked its way into my lungs. I yearned to spend the next thirty-six hours with him, maybe more.

"On Saturdays, I usually go on a hike. Would you like to join me?"

My heart did a twirl. "Absolutely. I just need to finish what I'm doing on this file. Maybe another hour."

"Then I'll stop by my room at the hotel and shower and dress for the day before I pick up breakfast. That should give you enough time."

"Perfect." And so was he. Those flashing eyes directed my way had me inside out and upside down—in the best of all possible ways.

Once he left, I put my head into my project and completed the tasks I needed to get done, then jumped into the shower. Rushing so I'd be dressed when he arrived back, I threw on a pair of jeans and found an old flannel shirt of mine in the closet that I put on over a tank top. My old hiking boots were just waiting to be worn again.

I heard the front door open before I had a chance to use the hair dryer, so I left it down to air dry.

"Good timing. I'm starving." I glanced at my new lover—*is that what I should call him?*—and my breath caught.

His dark hair was also still wet, and the back curled up a little over his collar. He wore black jeans that hugged muscled thighs and a flannel shirt over a tight, long-sleeved, gray T-shirt. My hands itched to run themselves over his hard stomach and toned arms.

I swallowed. "I'll clear off the table." I needed to busy myself to get my thoughts off ravaging him yet again.

"Leave it in case you need to look at something later. We can eat at the counter."

He placed the bag on the granite surface and went into the kitchen to grab plates. Like he belonged. *Perfect.*

I dug the sandwiches out of the bag and placed one on each plate. "Where do you want to hike today?"

"Since you haven't been here in a while and this is your territory, why don't you choose?"

"How about Comet's Trail? The river is nearby. It's so pretty there." I'd shoot some photos on my phone to remember this day. To remember him. "I can't believe I'm taking a day off to go hiking. I usually work on Saturdays."

"Isn't that the beauty of living and working in a

small town? Things are much more laid-back. People enjoy a slower pace of life. It's why I've been spending more time here than in Chicago, even though I could have gone home while waiting for the permits."

"I've also been enjoying my time here." I bit into my sandwich, savoring the melted cheese over scrambled eggs. But seriously, dry toast would have tasted delicious if I were sharing a meal with him. "Taking a break during the day and heading to Hannah's for coffee or walking to the municipal building and talking to people along the way instead of sitting at my desk and picking up the phone. In San Francisco, I would have never stopped in at the newspaper office to share a story, which I did when you agreed to sponsor the fireworks. Whenever I'm out and about, I've been running into business owners that I've known for years. It's so nice to be able to breathe, to have a conversation without cutting a person short because I don't have time to talk." I took another bite, famished after a night of burning a significant number of calories. "So what have you been doing while waiting for the permits?"

"Looking into other potential projects here in Wylder, as well as in Cheyenne and some of the other small towns in the area."

"Have you shared information on these prospective properties with your dad?"

"He knows I'm looking, but he's waiting to see what happens with the hotel before he'll make any commitments. But I want to be ready to move once the hotel is finished. That's how sure I am of its success."

His confidence, as well as everything else about him, was an aphrodisiac. If the hotel was a success, and if his dad bought into his proposal to renovate others in the area, what exactly did that mean in terms of his residence? The only way to find out was to ask the direct question. "Is your plan to stay here in Wylder?" I glanced at him to assess his facial expression along with his words.

"I don't know. That will depend on how things pan out." He caught my gaze with his. "What about you? Have you even considered taking over the practice?"

Getting lost in the intensity of his eyes, I had trouble responding. The seriousness of his question didn't help either. This wasn't the first time he'd suggested I come back. Almost as if that idea would take root and grow inside of me. Perhaps it was working because I didn't want to dig in and give my stock answer this time. Those words would shut him down, and I'd lose my fantasy about taking things further with him. "There's always the possibility, I suppose. I haven't had much time to think about it." My evasive answer made me wonder if I was in fact softening my stance.

He sat back, studying my face. As if trying to read my mind. "I know you struggled with coming back home over the past few years because of your sister. And I've heard you loud and clear that now that your father's gone, you missed your opportunity to work with him. But you'd have a great career here if you did take over. I've seen how you interact with the townspeople. They love you. You're one of them. And they clearly trust you to step into your father's shoes."

Everything he said was true. In the past, my steadfast loyalty to Ashley had prevented my move. My father's death, in my mind, had sealed off that possibility forever. But maybe…under certain circumstances…

"Are you trying to persuade me to stay?" I flinched at my far-too-serious question and turned it into a tease. "Did my mother put you up to this?"

His rich chuckle tugged at my heart. "No. Merely having a conversation with you."

I surmised he had more to say on the subject, but instead he stood and cleared the counter, his smile disappearing. "Let's get going. It's a beautiful day."

Chapter Fourteen
Dylan

I shouldn't have started anything with her. But she was like a river flowing to the sea, and fighting the pull of her tide was impossible. Last night her sexual current had crackled around me from the moment I entered the Five Star. Fleeting touches, smiles that reached deep-blue eyes, her floral scent, and private conversations meant only for me converged and formed an arrow heading straight to my heart.

I couldn't stop myself from recommending a quieter spot. I definitely couldn't stop myself when she'd suggested her place.

We walked the trails in silence, enjoying the peacefulness of our surroundings, punctuated by birdsong and new foliage rustling in the spring breeze. I was too far into my head to emerge. Maybe she was too.

Was last night a mistake? Maybe. But I'd never forget the power of my emotions as I made love to her. How could it hit me so fast? Like a lightning strike singeing my heart with her initials, I was branded.

I could only hope she was too.

After an hour and a half, we came to a clearing by the river.

"Let's sit for a while," I offered. I wanted to talk to her. But about what?

She'd think me crazy if I admitted my feelings for her. We sat on a fallen log, and I pulled water and protein bars from my backpack.

I started with something trivial. "How long have you and Amber been friends?"

She took a long drink before answering. "Since ninth grade. We met in Mrs. Thimble's class, became inseparable, and remained friends even after I moved."

I loved how she remembered her teachers' names. They meant something to her. "Has it been hard to keep in touch? You two are living very different lives."

She took a bite from her protein bar. "We obviously don't see each other much, but we make it a point to get together at least twice a year. Amber visits in San Francisco every summer, and I see her when I come home at Christmas and other holidays. We also talk on the phone or text sometimes."

If that was her definition of a good long-distance relationship, albeit with a girlfriend, I was doomed. Even seeing her once a month wouldn't be sufficient.

"It looked like you two were deep in discussion last night at the Five Star."

Her forehead furrowed. "My mom told me that Amber had gotten engaged recently. Even though we'd spent time together at her store the other day, she'd never said a word. And she hadn't called to tell me." She shook her head. "We usually tell each other everything, whether significant or not, so I was puzzled."

"Did she say why she'd kept it from you?"

"Part of it was because Zach used to be my sister's boyfriend in high school. Although it was years ago, and of course Zach had no choice but to move on, she felt uneasy about telling me."

"Small towns certainly have a lot of land mines. Does it bother you that they got together?"

"No. They're both great people. They should be happy, and if they make each other happy, that's a plus."

"What was the other part of the reason?"

"She and Zach started dating after my father died."

"Two months ago?"

She nodded. "She was afraid I wouldn't approve of such a quick engagement. I'm not sure why she thought I'd be so judgmental. She's my friend. I want her to be happy. And by the looks of it, both of them have fallen fast and hard."

"Do you believe love can happen that fast?" I held my breath, waiting for her answer.

"Absolutely. Do you?" Her solemn eyes held mine, as if to search the depths of my being.

My heartbeat raced with my confession. "I do." I almost blurted out my true feelings for her, but she continued.

"Perhaps you may want to think about those land mines before making any final determination about living in a small town." She hastily added, "If that's what you're thinking."

She smiled, and it beamed straight to my soul.

"There is one thing that would weigh heavily in my decision to settle around here." Did I dare say it out loud?

"What's that?"

"A good lawyer."

She laughed at what I suspected she thought was a joke. "I'm sure that, once a sale goes through, you'll be well represented by the buyers."

Not what I wanted to hear. "My father has been in my ear about switching attorneys. I just had another conversation with him this morning after I left your place."

Her eyes lowered, and her shoulders sagged. "I was hoping you'd stay on as a client—as well as all my father's other clients—so there's a business worth something to sell." She turned toward me, her eyes bright. "Bryce will be there, and I'll be helping him from San Francisco behind the scenes until a bigger firm buys the practice."

My stomach knotted at her plea. But she wasn't taking the bait. I had to push her harder. "If you're not even considering staying, I'll have to evaluate my options. I don't know if I can risk the time to wait and see who buys the firm."

She inhaled as if taking in the strength she needed to deal with my possible defection. "Of course. I understand. I appreciate that you hung in as long as you did. Thank you."

My heart squeezed. Her unselfish recognition was going to make it impossible to leave the firm—at least while she was still involved. I could always switch firms if I wasn't thrilled with the buyer.

She continued. "When I met with Sam Emerson the other day to discuss a sale of the firm, he said it will probably take months, even longer, to find the right buyer. I plan to come back and forth to help out with the workload when I can."

If I remained as a client, at least I would see her once in a while, and maybe, just maybe, I could water the seeds of possibility during her visits.

She nudged me with her elbow, a playful gesture, but all lightheartedness had fled within me at her dogged insistence to sell the practice.

When I didn't respond, she leaned into my shoulder. "I can't talk about this anymore. We're spoiling our day off."

Simply feeling her weight against me flicked away some of the angst that had settled in my chest.

"This view of the mountains is one of my favorites, especially this time of year." Her voice curled around me, encouraging me to ditch the remaining melancholy. "The peaks are still snowcapped. I love how their shadow reflecting off the river makes it look like they are so close we could touch them."

As I studied her profile, she turned toward me, and I got caught up in her mesmerizing gaze. Hunger took over, and I leaned in and covered her mouth with mine as I threaded my fingers in her long, silky mane. My tongue teased her full lips open until I could revel in her sweet arousing taste. Her hands crawled up my chest and around my neck, pulling me closer. But we were on a log in the woods, no comfortable spot to be had.

I broke the kiss and laid my forehead against hers. "I'd be happy to cut our hike short and head back to your bedroom. Or mine."

She exhaled. "You're on."

Chapter Fifteen
Emma Jane

We spent a blissful afternoon in bed and had dinner with my mom at the house at seven. Mom already knew Dylan as one of my father's clients. She had met him on several occasions around town and was effusively thankful for his sponsorship of the fireworks for the Spring Festival.

What she didn't know was that I was falling for our festival savior. Although my mother would have to be blind to not see our furtive looks, stealthy touches, and ridiculously cheery smiles.

And of course, he followed me to my cottage when dinner was over.

Sunday was as idyllic as Saturday. We canoed on the lake, had a picnic lunch in the park, kissed, touched, hugged, and talked—attempting to learn everything about each other in a twenty-four-hour period.

I felt the clock ticking. I had eight more days before I was supposed to be back in my San Francisco office, and possibly an additional ten days if I could finagle them in order to appear at the planning board meeting. That would never be enough.

I was sliding fast from intrigue into love and didn't know how to stop myself. Nor did I want to. This feeling of free fall was magnificent, and the serious moments between us squeezed and tugged at my heart.

The week sped by with file reviews, working with the accountant to evaluate my father's business, and an inordinate amount of chitchat with clients. Whoever had an appointment spent at least a half hour discussing their family, their work, my family, my work, and the Wylder community. There was no getting around it, so after the first few meetings, I stopped fretting that I was wasting time and learned to enjoy the civility of it all.

Every night I saved for Dylan. We had dinner together in or out of town, then ended up in my bed, unable to separate until we had to begin a new day.

Whenever the heartbreaking thought of my impending return to San Francisco invaded my essence, I struggled to tamp it down. No use in despairing over it while I should be enjoying and savoring every moment. Besides, maybe Lynne would give me the additional ten days I planned to request.

Who was I kidding? She was difficult in the best of situations. Requesting time off no matter the circumstance was always met with resistance. Case in point—this two-week leave. In the six years I'd been at Carter, Masters, and Smith, I'd taken one week off a year even though I was entitled to four.

By Friday I had procrastinated long enough, so I picked up the phone and called my boss. But no amount of begging softened Lynne's stance on the matter.

If I wasn't back by Tuesday morning, I was fired.

****

"Hey, Bill. We're here to take over for you." I stepped up to the ring-toss game at the Spring Festival—with Dylan a few feet away in deep conversation with the mayor.

"EJ, so good to see you again." Bill shook my

hand. "I'm going to make an appointment with you next week to incorporate my business."

"What business do you have?"

"I started Wylder Realty with my brother. We opened it a few months ago. The real estate market has really been picking up around here. I guess city folks are finally seeing the benefits of coming to a less-populated area."

"Congratulations on the business. I'd be happy to talk to you about it. Make an appointment for Monday, and I'll go over the options with you." I was cutting it close since my flight was first thing Tuesday morning.

Dylan's hand settled on my hip, and heat ran up and down my body.

"Dylan, this is Bill Connolly. Bill, Dylan Addison."

"So you're the new owner of the Wylder Hotel. Nice to meet you."

I added, "I went to school with Bill's brother Kent."

Dylan chuckled. "Of course you did. I think you have a connection to everyone in this town. If you didn't go to school with them, you did with their sibling or had one of their parents as a teacher or coach."

Bill jumped in. "That's how it is here in Wylder. Hey, Dylan. You should stop by our office. I can show you what's available in case you want to open a satellite office for Addison Redevelopment."

Dylan's expression was unreadable. "Thanks, Bill. I will. Here's my information." He handed him one of his business cards.

Bill scanned it. "You're staying at the Vincent House? Aren't you going to buy a house around here?

Or are you planning to move into the hotel once it's up and running?"

"I'm not sure. But if I decide to settle around here, I will definitely need your services."

I felt his glance as he pulled me closer.

We no longer hid our affection for each other. Once my mom confronted me the day after we had dinner together about the fact that we weren't fooling anyone, we let it go. Why hide our relationship despite its upcoming expiration date?

We switched places with Bill and took over the game, teasing the older kids and coddling the younger ones. A steady stream of acquaintances welcomed me back, and I'd given up my refrain that I'd only be here for a few more days. No one seemed to think my leaving would be permanent anyway, no matter what I said, and it only made me sad when I repeated it.

I introduced Dylan to everyone who came to our stand, and he started to relax into the comradery of Wylder.

"This is a nice town you have here," he said during a lull.

"You're the one who picked it." I sidled closer to him, needing his touch. "When I was a senior in high school, I couldn't wait to leave, at least for a while. Even before Ashley died, I wanted to experience a big city and get away from the negatives inherent in small towns. In coming back for these two weeks to work instead of just visit, I now see how a town like this could be charming."

"Does that mean you're considering moving back?"

I studied his face. "Why are you asking?" Only one

answer would allow me to consider.

He moved into my space, delicately caressing my cheek, sending zings and sparkles through my blood. I connected with his gaze, those crystal-blue orbs deadly to my concentration but life-giving to my soul.

His Adam's apple moved up and down in his throat. "Because I'm falling in love with you and I don't want you to leave."

My head swirled, and my heart jumped. Emotion clogged my chest. "I'm falling too," I whispered, afraid to give voice to such an absurd but real emotion.

"Hey, you two, break it up." Mayor Tim stood outside the booth. "I'm ready to win this game for my daughter." His arm wrapped around his child's shoulders with parental affection and tenderness.

I stepped away, sliding my hand over Dylan's arm, savoring our connection. "Here you go." I handed Tim five rings in exchange for a ticket, then lowered myself to his daughter's level. "What's your name?"

"Kirsten." A shy smile inched over her lips, showing a missing front tooth.

"My name is EJ." I winked at her. "Let's see if your daddy can win you a stuffed animal. Do you think he can get a ring over one of these bottles?"

"Yes. My daddy's the best."

Dylan cheered him on, giving the appropriate dejected sighs when he missed. On his third round of rings, he succeeded, and Kirsten leapt up and down with her hands over her head before hurtling herself into her father's arms.

What a sweet and endearing sight—a portrait that tugged at my heart. Would I ever have that?

"You won, Daddy!" Admiration beamed from her

face.

"I did. For you, honey. What would you like?" He picked her up so she could point to the stuffed animal she liked best.

She chose a multicolored kitty that looked like it could also be a dog or a bear or a mouse. Hugging it tightly, her other arm thrust around her father's neck, she looked over at me. "I hope he can win one for you." She glanced at Dylan.

I shrugged. "I don't know. He might not be as good as your daddy at this game."

A line had formed again, so Tim and Kirsten left with their prize. I stole a moment to study Dylan. I so wanted time to explore the profound words said between us, but we had a job to do. Yet those words lodged in my every cell and atom, sparking a happiness that couldn't be contained.

During a short break while my mother relieved us, we roved the grounds, stopping to chat with whomever greeted us. The mood was celebratory, and everyone seemed to be enjoying the food, the weather, and the spirit of community.

"There's Adam Colten," I whispered, grabbing his wrist. "Let's go talk to him. Make sure there's no hidden agenda the night of the planning board meeting." I walked into Adam's path. "Hi there." I brought out my sunniest smile. "I'd like you to meet Dylan Addison."

The men shook hands, and Adam even grinned. "Nice to finally meet you, Dylan. You have quite a persistent lawyer on your side."

Dylan glanced at me, then back at Adam. "Yes. I'll only work with the best."

I spoke up. "Have you heard any grumblings about our request? I'd like to know what I'll be walking into on June second." I had already shared the bad news with Dylan that I had to return to San Francisco but promised to come back for the planning board meeting.

"I'm sure you'll find a way to win over the board, even if they do have objections." His tone had turned hard. Not good.

"Adam, I really appreciate your help in getting us on the next agenda. I hope you and I can put the past behind us." It might take more than a few judicious words to assuage his long-term memory.

"We shall see. Good luck at the meeting." Then he turned and left.

"What was that all about?" Dylan's brow furrowed.

I exhaled a long breath. I might as well share my embarrassing past. "During senior year, I was on the debate team. Adam was too. We were on a winning streak at various competitions throughout the state. During the state championship, I went over the time provided to do research on an issue, and our team was disqualified." The sinking lead in my stomach, although a little less daunting than back then, still made an appearance. "Most of the team was supportive, saying it could have happened to anyone. And they knew I was still reeling from Ashley's death. But being Hank Hampton's daughter and the star of the team, I was humiliated and embarrassed beyond limit. As if it weren't bad enough that the entire school learned about my blunder, an article appeared in the paper the next day. The whole town read about it."

My face burned with shame. "After that, I always wondered, if I did return here to practice law, would the townspeople think I wasn't in the same league as my dad? He was a master mediator, a thoughtful advocate, and loved by all. Even his adversaries. I was afraid I wouldn't be able to rise to that level of esteem. Being Hank's daughter, I'd be elevated to a position as his partner that I didn't deserve."

"That was a long time ago, EJ. Certainly, the people of this town wouldn't hold an error made at eighteen against you now, especially given the tragedy you had suffered."

I exhaled. "Adam Colton is still carrying a grudge, and I can't seem to find my way around it. He seems to be the only one, though. I haven't felt it from anyone else. But don't worry, he's not on the planning board, although he'll be at the meeting." My job between now and then was to get on his good side. I didn't want to leave anything to chance in Dylan's permit hearing.

"Maybe I should have hired a lawyer who has friends in municipal government." His eyes flashed with playful mischief.

"You did. My father. Then you inherited me."

He snaked his arm around my shoulders and hugged me close. "I'm glad I did, or I wouldn't have gotten to know you."

His affectionate words curled around my heart and wrapped it in warmth. "Thanks."

"You were smart to get experience outside of the watchful eye of the community. Now that you're back—for whatever time—it's clear that your advice is sought and respected. That's been my problem in working with Addison Redevelopment. I started right after college, getting my MBA at night. Everyone who worked there assumed I had gotten the position I had because I was the son, not because I deserved it."

His arm tensed. "I worked hard to overcome that stigma, but it was impossible to conquer. My two brothers never even tried to work for the business. I guess they were smarter than me—wanting to make it in the world on their own merits. That's why I started to travel around, looking for opportunities for the company outside of Chicago. It got me away from the scrutinizing eyes that searched to find fault with the boss's son, even if there was none to be found."

The ear-piercing squeak of a microphone interrupted our conversation. Mayor Tim stood on a platform where bands had performed throughout the day.

"Thank you, everyone, for coming out and celebrating at our Spring Festival."

Roars, cheers and claps ensued.

"We've been lucky to have the perfect weather to get out and commemorate this beautiful season. I want to thank our co-chairs, Gloria Hampton and Beth Conti, for their hard work and dedication in pulling this event off. It wasn't easy given the restrictions on our town budget this year, but with all of your support in volunteering and sponsoring events, I must say this is probably one of our best celebrations."

He looked out over the crowd. "There is one person here who is new to town, and I'd like you all to give him a warm welcome when you meet him. Dylan Addison. He recently bought the Wylder Hotel and is in the process of renovating it. It will be a beautiful space for all of us to hold our special events and for outsiders to stay in while enjoying what Wylder has to offer. Hopefully, the hotel will be open by the fall." He paused to allow his words to settle in while the audience applauded. "One more thing and then I'll let you get back to enjoying the festival. Dylan and his company, Addison Redevelopment, have generously sponsored the fireworks for later this evening."

The crowd erupted in applause again, and those in the area turned to thank Dylan personally.

I was thrilled that Tim had given Dylan this shout-out. The mayor's kind words would help pave the way for him to become fully immersed in the community while also advising the members of the planning board to get this project moving. A win-win.

Dylan leaned in and whispered in my ear, sending tingles through my blood.

"How much am I going to have to pay for that great piece of PR?"

I chuckled. "You already did by sponsoring the fireworks. But getting the mayor's seal of approval came from you being friendly with him as well as others in this town. You never know who's going to be talking about you, so don't piss anyone off. And continue building on your goodwill."

"Great advice. Now if only I can live by it."

We worked side by side at the ring-toss booth until nine, at which time the fireworks started. It was a magnificent display that had the entire town oohing and aahing, thanks to the amazing man who stood by my side.

****

On Monday morning, Sam Emerson stopped by my office. "Your mom did a great job with the festival on Saturday. Everyone's been talking about it."

"It was better than I remembered it, and I loved it

back in the day. Mom and Beth are amazing."

"I'm assuming you had something to do with getting the sponsorship for the fireworks."

I smiled. "Maybe a little."

"You're still a Wylder girl at heart."

His words warmed my soul. "Maybe I am."

"I came by to tell you there's an offer on the firm."

"What?" I couldn't have heard him correctly. It had been less than two weeks since I spoke to him about putting out some feelers.

"A mid-size firm in Cheyenne is looking to open a satellite office here. Of course, they knew of your dad and his great reputation. My partner, who's working with you on the business evaluation, shared with them the initial value of the business. They're willing to buy the building and practice for two million, if all the clients stay. If clients leave, the price will be adjusted accordingly."

I swallowed. Wow. That figure was over what I'd expected. Little hammers beat at my heart, turning the ache of selling off a huge piece of my father into a piercing pain. "That was fast." Too fast for me to welcome the offer with open arms. "I need to talk to my mother about it. She's the beneficiary under my father's will."

"Of course. But don't wait too long. This firm is looking at other small firms in the area as well."

I stood to walk Sam to the door, my legs unsteady, my head fuzzy. "Thanks for stopping by. I'll speak to my mom today."

As soon as he left, I closed my office door, then sank into my desk chair while fanning my face. Heat swarmed over perspiring skin, and I feared I'd faint.

And not because of the great offer.

My father had built this practice over the past twenty-five years. It was an institution in Wylder. If Mom went ahead with the sale, this building would no longer carry the name of Hank Hampton, Attorney at Law. I thought back to the sign I had found in the cottage closet. And it would never be Hampton and Hampton.

Unless I came back.

If I did, I could rename it Hampton and Hampton as it was always meant to be. A legacy to my father and a declaration of my commitment to this town.

But was that what I wanted? Until this past week when Dylan and others had been seemingly planting seeds of possibility in my head, I hadn't even entertained the notion. Especially once my father died. Even now, with Dylan potentially in the picture, it seemed more of a fantasy than a reality.

Too many obligations filled my plate. Not the least of which was explaining the deal to my mother and, if accepted, writing to every client to advise them of the sale while convincing them to stay with the firm. All while working in San Francisco.

I inhaled, pushing it all aside for now and jumping into the slew of appointments I had in my calendar for today. My goal had been to help as many people as possible before I left. After today, I'd promised Bryce I'd do what I could from San Francisco to lessen his load while waiting for a buyer. Now that wouldn't be necessary.

My final day in the office flew by. At four thirty, after my last client, I headed to my mom's house to deliver the news.

"Hi, Mom. Have you recovered from the festival?" I walked into the kitchen, legs wobbly and heart heavy.

She sat with dozens of bills, receipts and other papers covering the table, a calculator front and center.

"Hi, EJ. Not yet. I'm tallying the net profits, which thankfully we have as opposed to a loss." Her smile lit up the room. Success could do that to a person. "What brings you here so early? I thought you'd be with Dylan your last night in town."

I sat across from Mom. "I have some good news for you."

My mother's questioning gaze mirrored my own seriousness. "If it's good news, why don't you look happy?"

Very astute. "Sam Emerson came by. He has a buyer for the law practice and the building." I kept as much emotion out of it as possible, refusing to label it as Dad's business. "It's a mid-size firm in Cheyenne that will keep the business running here. Hopefully, they'll keep Bryce and Carol on and send in other attorneys to help."

"Is the offer too low?" My mom's eyes held the same sadness I felt.

"No. It's an amazing offer. Two million. If all the clients stay." I thought her face would light up. But it didn't. "Were you expecting more?"

"No, no. I…feel…I don't know. A little depressed about letting it go." Her heavy sigh echoed around the room. "I know I asked you to sell it." A tear slipped down her cheek.

Oh no. I had been so close to the verge of crying myself that seeing my mom's lonely tear flooded my eyes.

I swallowed my misery. "We need to let Sam know as soon as possible. You don't have to make a decision right now, but the firm is looking at others, so don't wait too long." I took my mom's hand. "I'm sorry."

I was sorry for so many things. That my dad had died too young, that I hadn't made the move to practice law with him, that my mother was suffering, and most of all that I couldn't say the words that would make her happy. That I would stay.

The reality of my city life—complete with house, a successful career, and friends—was pulling at me from one end. And the fantasy of small-town life—with my mom, my dad's and sister's memory, the Wylder community, and the brightest star, Dylan—was pulling at me from the other.

A huge decision such as this couldn't be made under pressure. And the pressure was on.

But my biggest fear strangled my soul. Would the fantasy disappear if I didn't embrace it now?

Chapter Sixteen
Dylan

I waited at our table at the Vincent House Restaurant, checking my watch frequently. It wasn't like EJ to be late. Something or someone must have detained her at work. Possibly one of her more talkative clients.

At six twenty, she came flying in. "I'm so sorry. I was at my mom's."

I rose from the table and kissed her cheek, inhaling her sweet scent as if it were my life's blood. "Is everything okay?"

She sat, avoiding my eyes. "Yes." But the tightness in her tone belied her response.

I motioned for the waitress to bring our drinks, which I had preordered—merlot for her and cabernet for me. Once the glasses were placed on the table, I asked the waitress to give us a few minutes.

"What aren't you telling me?" I took her hand and massaged her palm.

"We have an offer on the law practice. Cromwell and Oliver from Cheyenne wants a satellite office." Her gaze connected with mine, and a well of sadness sprang within.

My breath caught in my throat. If the business was sold, that would be the end of us. Unless I moved to San Francisco—not part of the small-town redevelopment plan I'd been selling to my father. I dared ask the question. "Why aren't you happy? I thought that's what you and your mom wanted. Is the offer too low?"

She shook her head. "It's a great offer."

"From an excellent firm." *My father may get his wish after all.* "Is your mom going to accept it?" My stomach clenched as I waited for the axe to drop.

"I assume she will. She was caught off guard, just like I was. It was so fast. I thought it would take months for Sam to find a buyer."

I studied her face, looking for a clue to key in to her state of mind. But I couldn't read her. "Have you thought more about taking over the practice?" It was now or never for her to make that decision.

She shook her head, her beautiful eyes clouding over. "It's not a decision I could make this quickly. I thought I'd have the luxury of time to consider it. Prior to coming home two weeks ago, it never occurred to me that it was something I would even contemplate now that my dad is gone. But these past two weeks have been eye-opening."

She took my hand and looked straight into my eyes. "You were instrumental in helping me see that Ashley is still a part of me and she's with me no matter where I am." The beginning of a smile inched over her lips. "Surprisingly, I've been happy representing the townspeople in doing their wills or helping them with their businesses. I've gotten involved in house closings and aiding clients in obtaining mortgages. Everything I've done in the past two weeks was really important to them."

She sipped her wine, glancing out the window

where a host of businesses resided in the town. "In San Francisco, my clients are faceless corporations buying and selling huge commercial real estate properties. Of course, I talk to the vice president in charge of whatever deal I'm working on, but it's not the same. It's not their money they're dealing with. It's a transaction—not a personal need." She fidgeted as if trying to find comfort in her words. "Still, it's what I'm good at. What I've built my career on. I can't walk away on a whim."

I wanted to push her to stay, to continue to enjoy the civility of helping real people with real problems. But she needed to come to that conclusion on her own. If I swayed her and she hated it, then where would we be?

"While I would love to weigh in on this issue, it's not my place. You have to do what's best for you as well as your mom. But I will say one thing. This town came alive for me over the past two weeks through you. You worked your magic and brought me into the fold. I've met so many people that I now feel like a part of this community. I have you to thank for that." I picked up my glass and gave her a silent toast.

"What's next once the hotel is renovated?"

"Hire a competent manager that I could trust so I can work on other projects."

"Which projects can take you anywhere in the United States." She was making a point. Very lawyer-like when I would have preferred a more personal discussion.

I chose my words carefully. "My goal is to focus in this area, although not necessarily Wylder. There are a lot of old towns that could use a renovated hotel." Honesty was key. And I wasn't going to put my heart out there by saying I'd consider Wylder as a home base. Especially since the one person I would make that decision for had both feet out the door.

I sipped my drink, the melancholy of our last night together settling deep. Yes, she'd be back in a week and a half to meet with the planning board on my behalf. But only because I insisted she represent me. She wasn't coming back to further our connection.

"Well, I guess this is it. Our last dinner together." I sought her eyes, hoping the overpowering bond between us would unleash a miracle and alter our paths.

She bit her lip, misery shadowing her beautiful face. "These past two weeks went by so fast. We...happened so fast." An understatement with an undercurrent that scattered skepticism over her true feelings.

"Are you questioning my love for you?" Hurt lanced my heart.

"No." She threaded her fingers through mine, usually a conductor of electricity but tonight a conduit of agony.

"Maybe it's best if we say good-bye right now." I hated myself for saying those words out loud, but I couldn't eat, and spending the night together would only bring more pain.

Her deep-blue eyes widened in surprise or maybe shock. "Please don't end it like this." She tightened her hold on my hand.

"What do you want, EJ? A long-distance relationship with you in San Francisco and me in this area? It's not solely geography that's separating us. You're choosing to represent big-city developers and their megadeals over helping the little guy or gal.

There's nothing wrong with that. But that's my father's track, not mine. It's what I've been working to get away from. I'm focused on making small communities better. You're focused on making big cities bigger."

I exhaled my frustration. "I'm not saying you shouldn't do what makes you happy. You should. But I fell in love with the woman who yells across the bar to order a beer or tries to convince the permit officer to let high school debate issues go. The woman who talks me into spending ten thousand dollars on fireworks to prop me up in this community and then has me work at the ring toss so I'll meet everyone she knows. And I especially fell in love with the woman who dances the two-step with me at the Five Star."

Tears brimmed in her eyes and threatened to spill over her dark lashes. I hadn't meant to make her cry. I only wanted to make her understand.

She nodded, then rose. "I have to go. I'll see you in nine days."

Then she left.

Chapter Seventeen
Emma Jane

For the next week, I worked twelve-hour days. A myriad of reasons kept my head down and my brain on overload. I had to catch up on the Briar closing, which had been pushed ahead two weeks and was happening on Monday. But I also needed to clog my mind so no thoughts of Dylan could enter.

I had fallen in love with him—that was clear. But the woman he had fallen in love with wasn't me. It was a two-week version of me. His words had hurt beyond reason. Whenever they floated through my consciousness, they stabbed my heart and pierced my soul.

Compounding that were the worries I couldn't seem to shake. Had Mr. and Mrs. Evans gotten their mortgage? Did Bryce make time to have the Petersons sign their wills? Were the incorporation documents filed for Bill Connolly and his brother Kent? A few times a day, I found myself sending an email to Carol to ask those specific questions and to give directions for other client issues that had invaded my brain.

Whenever I could spare a moment, I spoke to Sam about the terms of the sale of my father's practice, negotiating on behalf of my mother to get the best deal possible. A contract would be sent to me by the end of the day next Tuesday for my review. If approved, my mother would sign it when I was in Wylder for the planning board hearing.

"I'm so glad you're back." Lynne flopped into a chair in front of my desk. Of course she was. She no longer had to handle the last-minute, day-to-day issues cropping up on the Briar deal. When I didn't respond, she continued. "Aren't you glad to be back? It couldn't have been easy dealing with all those petty issues prevalent in a small-town practice. You probably couldn't wait to get out of there."

I put my pen down. "It was actually a lot of fun. I never thought I'd say that about the practice of law. But talking to my father's clients—and exchanging information about their families and mine—was like a breath of fresh air. People there care about each other. Everything isn't a business transaction. A transfer of money. I was representing a young family who was buying a house before their baby was born. They couldn't get a mortgage for the entire amount due. So the sellers took back a mortgage for the balance. Not because they couldn't find another buyer, but because they wanted this young family to enjoy the house they had raised their children in."

"Oh brother. That sounds a little too Walton-y for me." Lynne's grimace underscored her sentiment.

"A few weeks ago, I may have agreed with you. But sitting here today, without a moment to grab a cup of coffee at the nearest diner, without a thought of stopping to chat with the owner of the pharmacy, or running into the mayor on the street and catching up, I have to say it was refreshing. And different. And fun. I bought some less-conservative clothes at my friend's boutique, I stopped at the newspaper office to garner some publicity for a client, and I worked at the ring-toss game at the Spring Festival."

"Did you do any real legal work while you were there?" she scoffed.

"I did. Plenty of it. And it made a difference to the people I helped."

"Well, you're making a difference to Ron Briar by closing this deal. I'll let you get back to it."

Apparently, she wasn't up for more Pollyanna tales of Wylder life.

And if I knew what was good for me, I wouldn't spend one more minute on that fantasy either.

****

My plane didn't arrive in Cheyenne until four on Wednesday. I was cutting it awfully close to the six-o'clock planning board meeting, but there was no use in getting to town earlier. Dylan said he would meet me at the municipal building, leaving no room for an awkward chat prior to that. As for seeing my mom, I'd have part of the day tomorrow to go over the contract at length and have her sign it.

At my insistence, the new firm had agreed to keep Bryce on as well as Carol, and they were both getting raises so their salaries would be commensurate with those paid in Cheyenne where the main office stood. While a little nervous about new management, both Bryce and Carol were happy they didn't have to find new jobs.

I took a taxi from the airport to Wylder and made one final stop at the office. The second Carol saw me, tears poured down her face, and I embraced her in a hug that meant so much more than good-bye. My own eyes misted as I squeezed her back.

"I'm sorry, Carol. I didn't think it would happen so fast." I stood back but held on to her hands. "It's a good firm."

"Everything is going to change." Her voice was thick with tears. And apprehension. "I know how those bigger firms work. Every little penny spent has to be approved by higher-ups, clients become numbers, and I'll have to attend meetings on everything from learning new computer systems to embracing the *culture* of the firm."

She was right. As my father's right-hand assistant, she'd made all the decisions from who got appointments when, to deciding on new client chairs in the reception area. She'd been the one who was really in charge, not my father. Of course, Dad had determined salaries and bonuses, but other than that, she'd had free rein. At larger firms there was a committee for everything—office furniture, quality of life, IT needs, diversity and inclusion. The list went on. And on. It would be a huge adjustment for Carol.

"I know it may not be easy at first, but once you get used to the transformation, it will seem like second nature. You may even have less responsibilities than you do now." I smiled weakly, knowing she didn't want fewer obligations. She simply wanted everything to remain the way it had been. "What does Bryce think?"

"He's young. He's just happy to have a job with the new firm. He'll adjust to the different systems much quicker than I will. And his day-to-day work won't change. He'll still be meeting with clients, drafting pleadings, and going to court."

"Is he in court now? I wanted to wish him well."

"Yes. He should be back soon. Do you need

anything for tonight's meeting?"

Ever the professional and forever loyal to my dad and therefore me, Carol looked hopeful, as if one more job under the old regime would make this send-off a little easier.

"Thanks, but I've got it all right here." I held up my briefcase. "I'm going to check my office to make sure I didn't leave anything behind or out of place."

I stepped into the hallway, taking in the scent of paper and old leather-bound books containing Wyoming case law, which lined the wall. The conference room was dark, every chair in its place and the table polished to a sheen. Bryce's office was a mess of files and paper surrounding a half-empty mug of cold coffee. Inching into Dad's office, I scanned the walls where his diplomas and certifications hung in dark-mahogany frames. Pictures of him and my mom attending various events populated one of the shelves on his bookcase while my law-school graduation photo stood as the centerpiece. Over to the right, closest to his desk, was a photo of me and Ashley the summer before senior year. We were at Lake Tahoe on vacation, standing on a dock, our smiles huge, our arms wrapped around each other's waists.

I sat at his desk and turned to see the photos—his view every day that he'd sat there—every day that he'd waited for me to join him. Tears poured down my face as I spoke to him.

I'm so sorry, Dad. If I'd known you were going to leave us so early, I would have come home. I would have been honored to practice law with you. To learn your special way of dealing with people. I swiped at my face to remove the tears, but more followed. *My steadfast loyalty to Ashley overshadowed my allegiance to you. I shouldn't have let it. But after years of procrastinating with excuse after excuse, I'd convinced myself that a small-town legal practice would be boring, unfulfilling. I thrived on the bigger stage where multimillion-dollar corporate deals seemed much more important than a piddly house closing. I told myself that the experience and the mentoring I was getting at one of the top firms in San Francisco was far more critical than the experience and the mentoring I would get from you.*

I was wrong.

You touched so many people with your sage advice, your gentle way, and your legal counsel. The mark you made on this town was so evident in the short time I was here trying to step into your shoes. Every person I talked to had a kind word to say. You accomplished things through working together with people as opposed to taking a position and cramming it down their throats. I chuckled at the conversation I'd had with Adam Colton that first day. He'd had the nerve to insinuate he would have given my dad the permits without a hearing, but he wasn't about to let me off so easily. *I bow to your talent, your collaborative ways, and your grace. I love you, Dad.*

I rose, trailing my fingers over his desk. I walked over to the bookcase and gathered the framed photos to take to Mom. Carol would pack the rest of my father's things before anyone moved into his office.

Then I entered my office. It was empty, just like the day I'd moved in. I had nothing personal to gather, nothing to pack up before another attorney took over the space. As if I'd never been here.

Aren't I more significant than this? "Absolutely," I said aloud, perhaps to assure I heard myself.

I glanced at my watch. I had to get over to the municipal building for the hearing.

"Carol, I'm heading over. Wish me luck." I smiled. "And don't pack up my father's office yet."

I left the building and strode to my destination, feeling lighter and freer and happier than I'd been in a long time.

****

The Wylder Hotel matter was listed fourth on the agenda. I sat on a metal folding chair among fifteen other people who either had applications before the board or had nothing better to do on a Wednesday night than sit through a boring meeting. I waved to several people I knew, but Dylan had not yet arrived.

Adam stood from his seat at the long table up front facing the attendees. "Let's get started. Drake, you're up. The board will hear from you with regard to your request to build a café onto your bakery."

Drake Fenley ambled up to a wooden dais placed in the middle of the aisle for applicants to use while pleading their cases. He droned on and on about the need for an extra two thousand square feet to add to his bakery so patrons could eat inside. I tuned out, every now and then glancing toward the entrance, awaiting Dylan. Where was he?

After a half hour of questions from the board and answers from Drake, his permit was approved. Next up was Lena Parker who wanted to add an addition to her dry-cleaning business. Another half hour—permit granted—still no Dylan. Had he decided not to come? It wasn't like he had to be here since he was represented by me, but he'd been so anxious that I assumed he'd be by my side, furiously writing notes to me about specifics—as if I didn't know his case by heart.

Halfway through the third case, I heard the door open and close. The air in the room shifted, and my heart hammered even before I turned to see that Dylan had finally arrived. I gave him a wave, and he nodded, but he didn't come to sit next to me. Instead he sat on the other side of the room. *Really?*

Our case was ultimately called at seven fifty. I stood and approached the dais, placing my folder on the stand. All eyes turned to me, including those in the audience. I addressed the board and introduced myself, as if I needed an introduction. I knew everyone on the board from growing up in town. After I gave my initial five-minute summary of our application, I was asked two soft questions. Then the board voted and approved the permits.

They had to be kidding. It couldn't have been that easy. I had left the office at ten that morning to get to the airport, go through security, wait over an hour at the gate, fly two-and-half hours, take a forty-five-minute taxi from Cheyenne to Wylder, sit through close to two hours of other permit application hearings, all for ten minutes?

Keeping my glare to myself, I looked at Adam. He merely shrugged.

I addressed the board. "Thank you for your time and for granting Mr. Addison's permits. Once renovated, the Wylder Hotel will be a thriving business, which will in turn drive business to others in town." I smiled at them, picked up my file, and left the room.

I waited in the hall for Dylan, who followed a few

minutes later.

"Hi." My nerves fluttered, and oxygen was in short supply.

"Hi," he said. No evidence of satisfaction over our win flashed on his face.

"I was surprised you didn't come earlier. I know how anxious you've been."

"I called Adam this afternoon. He told me we were fourth on the list and I didn't have to get here until seven thirty."

I should have thought to do the same thing, but I'd been looking forward to seeing Dylan, even if at a tedious planning board meeting. Apparently, he hadn't felt the same way about seeing me.

"It seems that you didn't need me here to represent you. The board had already made up their minds to grant the permits before I even started talking."

"The work you did behind the scenes leading up to today surely paved the way. I didn't want to chance it, though. Thanks for coming. Send me your bill." He turned to leave.

My stomach fell, and I reached out to stop him, but he was already near the front door.

"Dylan, wait." My voice was loud with desperation.

He stopped but didn't turn.

"I'm going to take over my father's firm."

Silence echoed around me as I stood in the tiled foyer of the municipal building, arm still outstretched. Waiting for my words to sink into his consciousness. Waiting for him to look at me. Waiting for him to gift me with his amazing smile.

Seconds piled on top of seconds. *Please, Dylan.*

Please turn. Please acknowledge my life-altering decision.

I walked slowly toward him, afraid to stir the air, afraid my movement would push him out the door. But he stood still. Silent.

Moving in front of him, I whispered, "I love you." Then I said it with my eyes, delving deep into his soul, telling him I was the woman he fell in love with. The intensity of my gaze struggled to reach into his heart, promising I would be his love for life.

The shadows cleared from his eyes. The walls he'd erected fell to the ground. He pulled me into his embrace, crushing me against his chest, covering my mouth with his, hot and passionate and hungry.

I was gone, flying into the stratosphere with the man I had fallen for in a mere two weeks. Then his words sent me even higher.

"I love you, EJ. Forever and ever."

Epilogue
Emma Jane

The grand opening of the Wylder Hotel had arrived, four months, two weeks, and a day after the planning board issued the permits necessary to renovate the hotel. A blend of old world and twenty-first century melded to make it a unique space, and I was so proud of Dylan for making his vision a reality.

It had taken forceful demands tempered with patience in dealing with his subcontractors, along with working side by side with them day and night. He'd purchased a house in Wylder as soon as I moved back, and although I still theoretically lived in the guest quarters behind my mom's house, I stayed at Dylan's most nights.

The law firm was thriving, calling for a second associate to help with our client load. Even so, I took the time to walk through town a few times a week to check in on my business neighbors, which brought in still more work.

Even Adam had softened. He'd asked me to help him coach the debate team at the high school without one mention of my need to follow the rules. It wasn't Berkeley Law, but mentoring those students held a special place in my heart.

Tonight, hundreds of people mingled in the lobby beneath a huge crystal chandelier spilling prisms of light onto the guests. The citizens of Wylder didn't often dress in their finery, but this celebration called for a step up from denim and flannel, and they'd risen to the occasion.

Dylan stood across the marble expanse, talking to an older man who looked a lot like him. I inched my way through the crowds and slipped my hand into the crook of his elbow. "The man of the hour. I've heard nothing but great comments from everyone in attendance. The townspeople are in awe."

He smiled at me, blue eyes flashing with satisfaction. "EJ. I'd like you to meet my father, Deacon Addison. Dad, this is EJ Hampton. The woman I can't live without." He pulled me into his embrace.

"It's so nice to finally meet you, EJ. Dylan has said amazing things about you."

"It's good to meet you as well. So what do you think about our small town?"

"Very quaint. With a lot of possibilities for renovation projects. Dylan has been in my ear about investing here and in some of the surrounding towns."

I beamed at Dylan before turning my attention back to his father. "Has he convinced you?"

"Absolutely." He placed his hand on Dylan's shoulder. "You've done such a great job with this hotel that I'm making you the vice president in charge of our new small-town acquisition division. Son, you clearly know what you're doing, and you have a passion for these projects."

"Did I hear you correctly?" His stunned expression proved he'd had no idea his dad was even considering this promotion.

"You did. Congratulations."

I threw my arms around him. "I'm so happy for you. It's what you've wanted. And you so deserve it."

He turned back to his dad. "I'd like to headquarter that division here. I don't want to work out of the Chicago office."

"You're in charge. If that's what you think is best, then I'm behind you." He chuckled. "I didn't think you'd be returning to Chicago. Especially once you told me about EJ. And now that I've met her, I don't blame you." Mr. Addison winked at me, then cast his arm over his son's shoulders and radiated pride.

"Thanks, Dad, for your faith in me. It means a lot. But if you'll excuse us, I want to talk to EJ about something."

Dylan took my hand in his and led me to the right side of the lobby where a large old-fashioned gold clock hung on the wall above an archway. He pointed at it. "This is a replica of the clock that was at the Biltmore Hotel in New York City from the nineteen twenties until the hotel was demolished in the early eighties. New Yorkers, as well as visitors, would tell their friends to meet them under the clock at the Biltmore. I want this to be a meeting place for the townspeople as well as tourists."

I admired the intricate metalwork encircling the timepiece. "I love it and the connections you want to foster. You've thought of so many little touches here that are meaningful. You're an amazing hotel owner." I stroked his cheek and got lost in his eyes.

He covered my hand with his, sending jolts of fireworks through my body.

"As the first couple to start this tradition, I want to make it memorable. But I need this to be a private moment, so please forgive me for not getting down on one knee."

All the air whooshed from my lungs, and butterflies danced and jumped in my stomach.

"Will you marry me, Emma Jane Hampton?" He pulled a diamond ring from his pocket and held it in his fingers. The magnificent emerald-cut stone sparkled in the overhead lights.

My hand trembled as he raised it to his lips. He looked into my eyes for an answer, and from the depths of his I saw hope and love and promise.

A tear trickled down my cheek. "Yes, I'll marry you. I love you so much it hurts."

He placed the ring on my finger, then kissed my palm. "I love you too, EJ. You changed my world when you made the decision to come back home."

Flashbulbs went off, and the photographer from the *Wylder Times* crowed. "This is the best hotel opening ever. And this photo of a proposal under the gilded clock should make it to the national wires. Thanks, Dylan and EJ."

Dylan shook his head, laughing. "I did not clue him in to this."

I chuckled along with him. "Even if you weren't thinking about the great press you could get for the hotel, I think that photo will make it explode. Now everyone within a hundred-mile radius will want to not only meet under the clock, but get engaged under its glow. What a brilliant piece of marketing."

The crowd that had seemed mired in their own conversations while Dylan spoke privately to me were now abuzz with the romantic event that had just occurred in their presence. Within minutes the press of bodies to congratulate us was staggering.

"So much for our private moment," Dylan whispered, sending sparks and flutters skittering through my core.

My entire being flooded with love. "We'll have a whole lifetime of private moments—if we want them. And if we don't, the entire town will be happy to celebrate with us."

I had made the best decision of my life when I chose to return to Wylder.

A word about the author...

Maria Imbalzano is an award-winning contemporary author who writes about strong, independent women and the men who fall in love with them. She recently retired from the practice of law, but legal issues have a way of showing up in many of her novels. When not writing, she loves to travel both abroad and in the U.S. Maria lives in central New Jersey with her husband—not far from her two daughters and granddaughters. For more information about her books, please visit her website at http://mariaimbalzano.com where you can also sign up for her newsletter.

If you enjoyed this book, please consider leaving a review at your favorite vendor or book site.

CPSIA information can be obtained
at www.ICGtesting.com
Printed in the USA
BVHW030858170622
640057BV00014B/239